EDITED BY

Liz Busby

COVER ART BY

Emily E. Jones

HEMELEIN PUBLICATIONS

Further Light: Science Fiction and Fantasy in the Latter-day Saint Tradition, issue 1 (Winter 2026)

The stories in this book are fiction. Any names, characters, people, places, entities, or events in these stories are products of the authors' imaginations, and any resemblance to actual people, places, entities, or events is entirely coincidental.

Although the publisher, editor, and authors have made every effort to ensure that the information in nonfiction works were correct at press time, and while this publication is designed to provide accurate information in regard to the subject matters covered, the publisher, editor, and authors assume no responsibility for errors, inaccuracies, omissions, or any other inconsistencies herein and hereby disclaim any and all liabilities to any and all parties for any and all losses, damages, or disruptions caused by errors or omissions, whether such errors or omissions result from negligence, accident, or any other cause.

Cover artist: Emily E. Jones
Cover art copyright © 2026 Emily E. Jones. Used by permission of the artist.

The Hemelein shield and stars H logo and "It's worth your time" slogan are trademarks of Hemelein Publications LLC.

Edited by Liz Busby
Cover Design: Joe Monson
Interior layout and design: Liz Busby

Published by Hemelein Publications, LLC., hemelein.com
First Hemelein printing, February 2026
Print ISBN: 978-1-64278-071-0
Ebook ISBN: 978-1-64278-072-7
ISSN pending

10 9 8 7 6 5 4 3 2 1

Cover artist: EMILY E. JONES is a freelance illustrator currently residing in northern Utah, after receiving her Bachelor of Fine Arts from Brigham Young University in 2022. She aims to enchant with a variety of both traditional and digital illustrations, many of them whimsical and fantasy-themed. Emily has always been an avid reader as well, and loves to tell visual stories based on the books that inspire her! Her favorite things are cats, pastries, not-too-long hikes, playing piano, and finding wonder in the everyday. Find more of her work on theartofemilye.com.

FEATURES

EDITOR-IN-CHIEF
Liz Busby

FICTION EDITORS
Ryan Fairchild, Nathaniel Givens, Jeanna Mason Stay, Joe Monson, Stephen Pulsipher

NONFICTION EDITORS
Ryan Fairchild, Stephen Pulsipher, Jeremiah Scanlan, Thomas Sorensen

POETRY EDITOR
DA Cooper

COVER DESIGNER
Joe Monson

Further Light, Volume 1 issue 1, Winter 2026 (February 2026). Published semiannually. Annual subscription $50.00 USD via Substack: https://www.furtherlightmag.com. Submissions accepted via website. For further details, please see our website.

Contents

FICTION

ESSAYS

POETRY

Editorial

A Center of Gravity for the Fantastic

IN SOME WAYS, THIS MAGAZINE began back in the fall of 2007 at BYU when I first took a course on the Literature of the Latter-day Saints. Though that class mostly centered around realistic fiction and poetry, as a proper nerd, I convinced my instructor to let me write my final paper about the history of Latter-day Saints in science fiction. I spent hours in the library digging into articles about Orson Scott Card and Battlestar Galactica, as well as discussions of Mormon cameos in novels by Robert Heinlein and Piers Anthony.* This was just as the pop culture world was becoming familiar with the name Stephenie Meyer and long before most people had heard of Brandon Sanderson. My brief glimpse into the world of the LDS fantastic electrified my imagination. I had grown up reading Card's novels and enjoyed the idea that he was one of us—as all minorities take pleasure in the hometown boy who made good—but until that point I had never really thought about the potential of science fiction and fantasy as a particularly Latter-day Saint genre.

For me, the connection was now clear: unlike the polygamy novels we

* The best article at the time was Michael R. Collings's "Refracted Visions and Future Worlds: Mormonism and Science Fiction." *Dialogue: A Journal of Mormon Thought* 17, no. 3 (1984): 107–16. There's also a fantastic reply from Orson Scott Card in volume 18, no. 2.

Ill: NASA, Wide View of 'Mystic Mountain' (2010).

read in class which seemingly dealt with only angst, complication, and doubt, or the devotional novels that skimmed the surface of what it meant to be a good Latter-day Saint, our fantastic literature was able to dive into the revolutionary perspective of the Restoration, the way that our unorthodox view on so many theological questions opened up an expansive space for human potential, to examine the implications of what it means to believe radically.

Every few years since then (at least it seems so to me as someone who had a vested interest), a major news outlet discovered the prevalence and success of fantasy and science fiction writing in Utah and felt compelled to investigate, often because a major motion picture based on a novel written by a Latter-day Saint was about to be released. These reports usually gestured at the uniqueness of our theology—our belief in other inhabited worlds, in modern revelation, in human potential and theosis—as somehow priming us to write about the fantastic. Some pointed to our conservative culture and saw genre fiction as hearkening back to a simpler time where our values were more accepted, avoiding dealing with the more realistic and depressing themes of "real" literature. Some even concluded that for people writing about aliens and magic, we were disappointingly boring and family-oriented and liked an inordinate amount of salt on our food.* Of course, there is truth to all of these things (especially the salt one—my grandmother kept a saltshaker in her purse for emergencies). But these outside perspectives never seemed to capture that vision I had glimpsed as an undergrad of how the fantastic could bring the Latter-day Saint theology from the background to center stage, giving the author and the reader room to really examine the immense possibilities and intense implications of the Restoration.

Of course, all through this

The goal of *Further Light* is to be a center of gravity for all things about Latter-day Saints and the fantastic.

time there have actually been Latter-day Saints—authors, fans, scholars—writing about how genre fiction illuminates the gospel and producing fantastical stories with a deeply Restorationist worldview. But

______

* Jason Kehe, "Brandon Sanderson is Your God," *Wired.com*, Mar 23, 2023.

their work has been scattered through various blogs, academic and literary journals, and fan websites. I could find them because I was constantly prowling the internet for just such things, but to the average Latter-day Saint, none of it was accessible.

This magazine was born out of a desire to have somewhere clear to send people when I talk about Latter-day Saints and speculative fiction and they ask where they can go for more. The goal of *Further Light* is to be a center of gravity for all things about Latter-day Saints and the fantastic. In these pages, we hope to move beyond the standard question of *why* there are so many Mormon characters in science fiction, and instead show *how* a science fiction story can be radically transformed when its Latter-day Saint characters are deeper than the aesthetics of a nametag and a smile. Instead of asking *why* so many LDS authors turn to writing fantasy, we will explore *what* we learn about the Restoration perspective on the divine by examining it through the lens of myth and subcreation. Instead of asking *why not* instead write something realistic and faith-promoting (as some unfortunately still do), we will unearth *when* Latter-day Saint speculative fiction actually got started by publishing works from earlier authors that show that Latter-day Saint fiction has in some ways always been speculative fiction.

Of course, selfishly, my hope is that the existence of this magazine will also incentivize the creation of new Latter-day Saint science fiction and fantasy, work that engages with the edge cases of our theological knowledge and pushes on the gap between our culture as it exists and as it needs to be. Speculative fiction is a great tool for asking questions that don't have tidy answers, and I believe that our work doesn't have to be didactic in order to take faith seriously. I hope that the weirdness of science fiction and the mythic quality of fantasy create a place where faith and complexity can exist side by side, where we can wrestle with the angels of the Restoration, where questions don't always lead to a loss of belief but a deepening of it.

The pieces in this first issue represent a wide range of genres, tones, and styles. They range from alternate history to magical realism, from an analysis of popular authors and streaming series to riffs on classic literature, from humorous and hopeful to dark and uncertain. As you read, I hope you find your mind and faith expanded and enjoy this first step in our journey towards further light.

- Liz Busby, Editor-in-Chief

Fiction

OPERA OF THE ABYSS

Part 1: Murder and the Rue Morgue

LEE ALLRED

October, 1902
Above the streets of Paris

LEANING AGAINST THE DUBIOUS cover of a crumbling chimney, Field Agent Nils Lund ejected the empty magazine of his Browning-Odgen automatic pistol and slapped in a new one.

The Paris slum La Vilette snaked in all directions, rooftops twisting maze-like limned but dimly by the sliver of moon. Streets below were lit not at all. The gas streetlamps of the La Vilette had been ripped up years before while residents awaited electrification. They still waited. French planning.

He racked the slide.

"I thought Paris was the City of Lights," Lund told his French associate who also served as his minder.

"And I thought Mormons had magic bullets," M. Dupin growled back at his Deseretan charge, knowing full well what bullets Lund had in his pockets. He'd frisked Lund often enough.

The fat, mustachioed Frenchman fumbled in the dark to reload the cylinder of his revolver. Some of that was due to the gun having to be loaded wrong-handedly; the cylinder on a Lebel swung out on the right side, the rifle-length 8mm pistol cartridges were long and clumsy to load. 8mm. Leave it to the French

Ill: Kevin Wasden

to be needlessly unique. The overly slender reed-like barrel of the Lebel made it look like a toy and it had the stopping power of a spit wad.

"I, at least, hit our prey," Dupin boasted, jamming the last round in.

Dupin had not, but what would be the point of arguing with the fat man?

As for the whipcord-lean Deseretan, Lund had grouped the entire contents of his magazine of ordinary copper bullets—seven in all—dead center into the thing they were chasing. Alas, his bullseyes had accomplished no more against the creature than Dupin's six wild misses.

That the Frenchman had missed was only to be expected. Dupin was an amateur, after all.

All of the secret agents of France's Rue Morgue were amateurs. Amateur part-time secret agents. The Rue believed that all that was needed to face down a supernatural menace was elan. Elan and simply being French. Training and proper equipment were superfluous.

Lund snorted. If French elan truly overcame all obstacles, the Rue would not have needed to turn to a hated Mormon for help—a Mormon agent trained up to the exacting standards of the independent Republic of Deseret's Correlation Department.

Lund peeked around the edge of the chimney. The creature was still on the next rooftop over, its great bulk blending into the thickening fog.

Down on the street, a cat screeched and a dustbin lid clanged. Shrill police whistles tweetled. Shoe leather slapped cobblestone, echoing in all directions. The flics—the Parisian police—undoubtedly rushing to-and-fro, blue serge cape aflutter, nightsticks drawn like cavalry swords for a charge and haring off after what they thought was the creature.

> # If French elan truly overcame all obstacles, the Rue would not have needed to turn to a hated Mormon for help.

"It's down on the street!" Dupin cried, trying to peer over the coping. He fumbled with his cased baton.

Now he's getting it out!

"The police have it cornered, *certainement*!" Dupin insisted.

"The police are chasing a cat, *certainement*," Lund said. The Frenchman was supposed to be a private detective of some note. Couldn't he even follow sounds?

"The creature will get away!" Dupin insisted.

Lund plucked the cased marshal's baton from the fat fingers of his French minder. The Rue Morgue marshal's baton was the sole piece of arcane equipment the French agency issued its agents. If Lund had used his baton on the creature earlier instead of his pistol, they might have just captured it then and there.

"It's not getting away," Lund said. He extracted the baton and tossed the empty gutta-percha case away. It clattered off the cobblestones down in the street, which would no doubt turn the flics back this direction in their snipe hunt.

One could only hope.

Lund gave the baton a couple practice strokes. It felt good in his hand. Solid. Fashioned well. Eighteen inches long and one inch thick. Plated with silver and chased with fleurs-de-lis. Underneath, the rod was iron. A very special iron. The same selenite meteor that Charlemagne's mystic sword Joyeuse was fashioned from. Much about the Rue Morgue was a sad joke; their batons were not.

He'd need it for what needed to be done next.

Ordinary bullets wouldn't stop the creature and Lund had been sent to France without the usual Departmental load out of runed rounds. The "magic bullets," as the Dupin had so sneeringly called them. Without access to arcane ammunition—Curse his boss for being right. Resupply, indeed!—Dupin's baton would have to serve.

Provided Lund could shake his watchdog.

The creature was fifty-feet straight ahead, crouching as Lund was behind a chimney. Lund could hear it scraping against the brick.

"Listen!" Lund exclaimed. "It is down in the street!"

Dupin, already distracted by the snatch of his baton, fell for it. He faced away from Lund and hung his whole fat face over the coping to stare downward into the dark.

Lund tensed his legs in just a certain way, activating the hidden springheel jacks on his boots. Tensile coils of rarefied air lifted him noiselessly a good thirty yards in the air. To Dupin, it would seem, once he turned around again, like Lund had simply vanished into the fog.

The Deseret agent landed catfooted on the other side of the chimney, less than an arm's length from his crouching quarry. Man-shaped the creature might be—seven feet tall and four-hundred pounds—but it was no man even though it wore an ankle-length greatcoat and an enormous floppy-brimmed hat.

Gaston Leroux. Or rather, what Gaston Leroux had become.

Lund stabbed the borrowed baton into the small of the creature's back. Blue eldritch lightning lit up the Paris rooftop.

###

One week earlier
Salt Lake City, Republic of Deseret

Nils had never liked the indoor firing range of the Department's Salt Lake headquarters. One of the sub-basements. In the yellow electric lighting, it felt cramped, confining, and the ventilation never scrubbed all of the powder residue out of the air.

"You're familiar with one of these," Llewelyn, the Department's armorer said rather than asked as he tossed a leather item Nils's way.

Nils caught it. It was a curiously-looking glove. Instead of covering the full hand and fingers, it had only finger loops, a wrist strap, and an abbreviated leather pad—like an archery glove only upside down. The pad fitted against the palm, not the back of the hand.

"'Palm of Gilead did I borrow,'" Nils mused.

"Yes, yes. 'Ere you left your room today,'" Llewelyn snapped. "They all say that. The question is, can you use it?"

"Never used on in the field. I've gone through the training course, of course."

"We'll see."

As Nils strapped the glove to his right palm, the armorer took the wooden box that Nils had just dumped all his Departmental field equipment in—his Combat Tactical Ring, his Liahomer, his pair of Coggles, and of course his issued .32 Browning-Odgen Pocket Hammerless automatic and a couple spare magazines—carried across the room, and locked it inside the gun vault.

Each of the locked-away items had been his constant companions in the field for years now. They were part of him. He felt naked without them.

Not that Llewelyn cared. "Begin," the armorer said. "Initialize the glove."

Nils concentrated and the glove became first translucent, then all-but-invisible. Intangible as well as it sunk right into Nils's hand and seemingly vanished all together. No arcane test that the Department knew of could detect it. It gave off no eldritch traces. The ultimate covert equipment item.

Llewelyn nodded. "Good, good. That's the easy part," he said. "Now try retrieval."

Nils concentrated again and the spindled brass ball of his Liahomer appeared in his hand, jumping the distance from vault to Nils without a care for Newton and his natural laws.

"Ouch," Nils said, shaking his right hand in the air. His palm burned from the arcane teleportation, like he'd pressed it against a red-hot stove. Red and tender but thankfully not blistered. Not yet. The bigger the object, the hotter the heat.

He repeated the performance for Coggles and ring, saving his heavy pistol for last.

"Now retrieve the spare cartridges," Llewelyn instructed.

"But I can't—"

"The magazines, if you would, Brother Nilssen," Llewelyn insisted.

Nils tried but failed. *Of course he failed!* The other items had saved his life numerous times. They were a part of him. Magazines, like spare rounds, were mere fungible items. He hadn't the emotional attachment to them he had the other items. The Palm of Gilead fed on that attachment, required it.

"Excellent," the armorer said, as if Lund's failure made him happy. He fetched the wooden box out and handed Nils back his fungible spares. "You're now to report to Room Seventeen."

Assignments. Lund disliked Room Seventeen even more than the armory.

###

Room Seventeen looked more or less like an ordinary business office. It was the man in Room Seventeen seated behind the desk that was far from ordinary: Nate Sabbas, the snowy-haired, mustachioed head of Deseret's Correlation Department.

A "pocket Mark Twain" some called the stern, leonine man. "A harsh taskmaster," others. Lund just thought of him as a tyrant, a tyrant in a good cause—that of protecting Deseret, the entire world, from supernatural threats—but a tyrant nonetheless.

Sabbas lifted open Lund's personnel file with the tip of his chewed pencil as if examining a dead fish someone left on his desk.

"Nils Lund," he read. "Born Telemark, Norway. Converted to Mormonism against the wishes of his father at age fifteen. Emigrated to Deseret against the wishes of his father at age fifteen. Changed his name to Lund prior to arrival for reasons unstated. Actual surname—"

"None of your business."

"—Nilssen. Father, Lutheran clergyman. Mother, deceased. Surviving brothers, three. Surviving sisters, two."

"Three."

"Our records have two," Sabbas said, looking up from the page, "with the third sister undoubtedly being none of our business as well." He resumed reading. "Speaks English with Norwegian accent, an affectation as this could be easily corrected by hypnogogic and is when on field assignments abroad."

"I'm not ashamed of where I came from."

"Only ashamed of whom." Sabbas closed the file. "The rest is a very tedious recitation of various Department assignments and commendations."

"Those assignments were hardly tedious." Lund had the body scars to prove it. The scars on his soul as well.

"Immediate supervisors note a stubborn tendency to kick against the pricks. There is stubborn and then there is Norwegian stubborn." Sabbas quoted from memory. He sat back and fiddled with his pencil. "Your Mormon God must love stubborn. He is busy gathering the stubbornmost of the world to beautify your pitiful desert. No one but the stubborn would attempt it."

"I see He's gathered you," Lund shot back.

"I was not *gathered*," Sabbas growled. "I was *sent*." By powers Lund hoped he'd never have the misfortune to meet, or so the rumors went.

The avowed atheist viewed all religions as equally nonsensical, Mormonism more so than any. Why such a contrarian, however nimble his brain might be, chose to serve as chief defender of the Mormon homeland was more than Lund could fathom. Lund could well believe Sabbas's muttered jest about being sent here against his will.

Sabbas grunted, reaching for another file folder. "Let us just hope that your stubbornness is stronger than the famed French intransigence."

"French?" Lund didn't like the sound of that. France was on the "no go" list of nations, just like the Confederacy. Borders closed to all Mormons. No diplomatic recognition of Deseret. Full trade embargo.

"Lund, I'm sending you on covert assignment to Paris," Sabbas said. "You're to retrieve a stolen item very similar to this." He opened a jeweler's box to reveal what looked like the mainspring of a pocket watch, only scribed with various runes.

"This is only a mockup I had run up locally. The real one required precision work so only one clock-maker in the entire world is capable of making one."

He snapped the box close. "*Was* capable, I should say. He was murdered, brutally torn limb from limb. The object was then stolen and taken to Paris to one Gaston Leroux. ATK job, we think."

First France, now ATK. This was why Lund had learned to hate Room Seventeen. This assignment had gone from bad to worse.

ATK, short for *Das Arbeiter-Thaumaturg-Kollektiv*. The Worker's Thaumaturge Collective: half Marxist political movement, half chthonic cult. The ATK used alchemy and terrorism to achieve its political aims. Led by the mad priest Rasputin, the

> **The avowed atheist viewed all religions as equally nonsensical, Mormonism more so than any.**

ATK had grown from a small rabble of crazies into an international power that threatened world order.

The ATK essentially ruled what was left of crumbling Tsarist Russia and were rumored to now hold sway over much of Germany and the Balkans as well. If the ATK was making a play now for France—

"Sir?"

"Answers first, questions later," Sabbas snapped. He tented his fingers. "I trust even a mind feeble as yours deduced that the little demonstration you were put through downstairs had a purpose. Showing is often easier than telling."

Sabbas got up from his desk and stepped to the large wall map of the Four Americas. Various colored pins were inserted into the map, noticing the location of supernatural menaces, dispatched and still outstanding, as well as the location of assigned agents. A few black flag pins—few yet far too many—marked fallen agents of the Department.

Sabbas plucked a black pin from where it had been stuck in the heart of the southern Confederacy and cradled it in his palm. He could have just as easily taken up a black pin from the Yankee North, the Republic of Texas, or Deseret herself.

"Eighty percent of our agents killed in the field died from logistics. Oh, monster or enemy agents killed them to be sure, but they died from simply running out of ammunition. Solution: remote resupply."

He stuck the pin back in its place of honor. "Obviously as you have just demonstrated, a Palm of Gilead is not the answer."

His swivel chair squeaked as he settled his elderly frame back down. "I'm told you have what passes for an education in this desert wasteland."

"Yes, sir. University of Deseret, Class of 1998. BA in Natural and Arcane Philosophy."

Sabbas snorted. To him, education came from doing, not from sheepskins. "Then it is remotely possible you have heard of 'selfsame.'"

"'Selfsame,'" Lund said, brow furrowed, trying to remember lectures from his college days. "A term for a widely debunked mystic ability to fashion a duplicate of one's self or of an object. The ancient Egyptians called such a *Ka*, the Chaldeans an *Aiwass*. Certain Tibetan mystics claim the ability today. This has not been proven."

"Your college textbook is out of date," Sabbas grunted. "I've seen it performed myself. By a practitioner of Psychognosis, it was. Very strange chap."

Very imaginary chap, Lund should think. Psychagogues and Psychagogy were only rumors and figments according to his professors.

"He could duplicate items, not people," Sabbas continued.

He blew out a puff of air. "Maybe even people in *his* case, not that he never showed me."

I bet not.

"At any rate," Sabbas droned on, "one of the gee-whiz boys in our laboratories thought he could create a selfsame device. Derivativaton, he called it." Sabbas shrugged. "Always promising the moon and delivering nothing but moondust, but if it meant resupply in the field, I was willing to order a prototype built. Hence the mainspring, without which the Derivativaton is an expensive paperweight."

Sabbas handed Lund a file folder. "Gaston Leroux, French reporter and Rue Morgue agent. Also, we believe, double-agent for the ATK. Indications are they offered him immortality in exchange for the mainspring."

Which meant he could very well be a struldbrug by now. A sort of reverse zuvembie. This had got from bad to worse to horrific.

"Be that as it may," Sabbas noted, "the stolen item was taken west to Paris by Leroux instead east to Russia. Possible internal struggle in the ATK? We don't know. Reports place Leroux in the La Vilette slums. Find him, recover the mainspring, avoid notice by the French authorities."

Notice by the French authorities would get Lund sent to Devil's Island—if not outright executed.

Sabbas glared at Lund from under his shaggy white eyebrows. "Under *no* circumstances are you to use or display Departmental equipment in Rue Morgue presence. Rouletabille would love to get his hands on our toys and copy them. You'll thus leave said toys here, taking only pistol and normal bullets."

Lund raised an eyebrow. "Normal bullets against an ATK struldbrug? Why don't I just slit my throat now?"

"You'll be allowed a Palm," Sabbas grudged. "Extreme emergency use only—and only if completely out of observation by the Rue Morgue. Your training alone should suffice against one lone struldbrug. If he is a struldbrug."

Sabbas pushed away from his desk. The briefing was over.

So too, probably, was Lund. He would be entering France essentially unarmed and stark naked with every hand against him.

Human or otherwise.

###

Paris, France

Lund travelled from Salt Lake to London via a circuitous airship route. London to Paris by British puddle-jumper dirigible. All under false Swedish papers. All routine, nothing Lund hadn't done a hundred times.

Only one oddity on the voyage: a bearded Persian fellow in an Astrakhan hat also aboard the puddle-jumper with him. He had an unusual combination of ebony skin yet piercing green eyes. The Persian followed him so closely aboard the airship—dining room to observation lounge, observation lounge to writing room—that Lund suspected the Persian for a moment of tailing him then shook his head at his own paranoia. A real tail would never travel with so striking a disguise. The art of covert tailing is to be utterly non-descript. If anything, it was as if the man were trying to make Lund notice him.

The dirigible locked its nose ring to one of the many mooring towers serving the busy Paris Aerodrome. Lund filed down the tower steps along with the other passengers. The odd Persian and his fur hat, after seeming to make sure to be seen, were soon lost in the crowd.

The custom shed was a madhouse of pressing bodies and Gallic temperament, and Lund immediately remembered why he despised France: pushy, rude, loud, and convinced they were the only civilized people in the world.

Frilly fashions, fancy foods, snooty buildings—all seemingly contrived to say "We French are better than all others." Straight Rameumpton stuff as far as Lund was concerned. Wide and Spacious Building.

If it'd been just that, he supposed he could let it go, but France seemed in intent on a race with its American protege, the Confederacy, on who could hate Mormons the most.

Southerners lynched any Mormon they found. France had dealt with the last openly French Mormon congregations as France had once dealt with the Huguenots. Massacres of entire local congregations, then reapplication of the Edict of Nantes to the few Mormons who'd survived the pogroms. Convert to Catholicism or die.

As Lund was mulling this over, a particularly surly specimen of French manhood, turned around to glower at Lund. "You stink of soap, *Angliche!*" he snarled.

Lund's retort regarding what the Frenchman stank of was interrupted by the press of a pistol barrel against his the back.. "No sudden moves, Monsieur 'Nilsson.'" The way the Frenchman hissed *Nilsson* told Lund his true identity was known.

> **France had dealt with the last openly French Mormon congregations as France had once dealt with the Huguenots.**

"This way," the voice hissed, the prod in his back directing him to a small room off to the side. "A nice friendly walk, two old friends."

Two old friends plus three or four rather useful-looking toughs with their hands under their jacket where pistols might be reached.

This parade of friends wound its way inside the room. Two more gentlemen awaited, both wearing cased marshal's batons depending from their waist belts.

Rue Morgue men.

One was bald, portly, mustachioed, and dismissible. The other was not. He was slighter and had the largest, roundest head Lund had ever seen. He had the face of a nineteen-year-old and the receding hairline of fifty. The elongated forehead suggested a massive cranial cavity, one put to use for La Belle France and her supernatural spy agency.

Lund recognized the round-headed man immediately: Joseph Rouletabille, head of the *Société de la Rue Morgue*. Rouletabille stood talking to yet a third man, that Astrakhan-hatted Persian. The Persian nodded at the Frenchman, collected a bundle of franc notes, and exited.

Lund had been shopped.

Paris boasted no actual street named the Rue Morgue. Rather, the *Société de la Rue Morgue*—like most government supernatural agencies—was named seemingly at random, whimsically so.

In matters arcane, true names are power, true names are dangerous. The working name of Lund's own organization—Correlation Department—signified nothing, just a name of convenience. Lund didn't know the Department's real name and he doubted anyone but Sabbas did. Maybe not even Sabbas. The Rue Morgue was the same—a name of convenience—and right now Lund wished he'd never heard of it.

He was taken via motorcar to a seedy-looking warehouse that must serve, if not as Rue Morgue headquarters, at least a field office. The stacked freight boxes were window dressing. The building's true functions happened in the upper loft offices where official portraits of King Philippe VIII and three-word slogans emblazoned the walls.

Long gone were the bloody revolutionists' heady cries of *Liberté, Égalité, Fraternité*. The restored July Monarch aimed to survive. France for monarchy, for Catholicism, for Frenchness itself. *État, Église, Ethnie* were the new French watchwords, and fanatics had been put in place to see that they were upheld.

Rouletabille's bully boys gave Lund a final frisk, patting him down for concealed items before shoving him down the corridor to the spy chief's office.

Amateurs! Had Lund been in their place, he'd have stripped his prisoner naked, torn apart his clothing stitch-by-stitch, and issued him replacement clothing.

The fools hadn't even examined Lunds boots other than feel for the top of a hidden knife—a good thing, as the boots were the one arcane item Lund had dared bring into the country.

Satisfied that Lund was disarmed, they took him to their boss. Rouletabille's office differed only in language and geography from upward like a spoiled child's. The round-headed man lit a foul-smelling French cigarette, and stubbed it out almost immediately. The dish-like ashtray on his desk covered in a score of similarly unused cigarettes.

"Just by entering the country," he continued, "I could have you sent to Devil's Island. I could have you shot this very minute."

"But?" Lund smiled mockingly.

There had to be a *but* or Rouletabille wouldn't be blustering like this.

The marble-headed spymaster gave a Gallic shrug. "Just so. *But.* There is a little service you might perform that would cause the *Société*

What we do have on the street of Paris is an inhuman fiend—an unearthly demon to be sure!

Room Seventeen. Maps on the wall. Flag pins on the map. A tyrannical protector seated behind the desk. The French spymaster's smooth complexion and rosy skin gave the illusion of youth; his hardened eyes betrayed him. That and the hard lines that edged out from the skinfolds around them. Those eyes blazed at Lund now.

"Did you think we French so incompetent, Monsieur Lund, that you thought you could simply waltz into France and we would not know?" Rouletabille's voice screeched to forget the little matter of your illegal entry and let you be about your *chasse au dahu*, your *quête futile* for your supposed ATK."

He savagely stubbed out another fresh cigarette. "*There is no ATK on French soil, monsieur!*"

Visibly calming himself, Rouletabille said, "What we *do* have on the street of Paris is an inhuman fiend—an unearthly demon to be sure!—slaughtering the residents of the slums of La Vilette in wanton fashion."

Rouletabille lit the last cigarette in the pack and actually smoked it for once, holding it in that awkward way the French handle their cigarettes and letting its blue-grey smoke curl past his face.

"Catch this demon for us and you may be on your way."

"He could have just asked, you know," Lund said, rubbing where the handcuffs had chaffed him. He stared at the wall map of Paris and the fourteen blood-red flag pins clustered in La Vilette.

"M. Rouletabille does not ask, he tells," said Dupin, the fat moustache who was heading up the investigation and who'd been assigned as Lund's keeper. Dupin was apparently a private detective of some local repute when he wasn't play-acting at being a secret agent.

Dupin, too, stared at the map. "I am of the opinion that it is a gorilla. One went missing from the Paris Zoo a year back. And strange hairs were found at some of the murder scenes."

"Gorillas don't talk," his peach-fuzzed assistant noted. The young man, boy really, was some sort of viscount, a twig of minor nobility. He was also a sop, a fob, and a histrionic Byronic. He was forever swooning, back of wrist to forehead, at the hideousness of the murders. "Witnesses said it talked."

"Witnesses are usually deluded fools who remember their imaginations,

not the facts," Dupin shot back, then shrugged. "In any event, my theory has been outvoted by M. Rouletabille. He believes it is a demon our priests have not yet managed to exorcise."

"I've yet to meet a demon," Lund said. "I *have* met a gorilla." It would certainly take something as strong as a gorilla to tear the victim's bodies like the photographs showed.

Lund bit his lower lip. "Let me see that list of victim names and addresses again." Two of those names were on Lund's mainspring theft suspect list.

Pretending he was studying the list, Lund casually added, "Tell me, did one of your agents go missing about a year ago. One Gaston Leroux?"

"*Sacré bleu!*" the boy sputtered. "How did you know? His body turned up but not his head! It was ghastly."

"It is also none of our guest's business, Raoul," Dupin said hurriedly. "It has no bearing on this case—"

"Except," Lund said, "that two petty criminals Leroux used from time to time are victims on your list." Criminals used to steal the mainspring and kill the clockmaker, according to Swiss police reports. "A third one still survives."

Dupin started. "Y-you think the purpose of this mad spree of killing was—?"

"To cover up the killing of Leroux's three confederates. Bury their murders under a mountain of

Ill: Kevin Wasden

random corpses." Lund turned back to the map. "You say there's a time pattern to these killings. When is the next murder due?"

"Tonight," gulped the boy.

"Then Jacques Grisot is a dead man. Unless we get there first."

October, 1902
Rooftops of Paris

Lund stabbed the borrowed baton, stunning the creature crouched on the rooftop. The creature spasmed upon the coruscating blue lightnings.

The coruscating discharge lasted only a moment. The rod's selenite ore stored up eldritch energies from nearby ley lines and discharged them on contact. Paris had only two weak ley lines—one under Notre Dame Cathedral, the other under the Paris Opera House—so the energies stored were weak and slow to recharge.

Once the crackling energies ceased, the monstrosity stood and whipped away its coat and hat in animalistic challenge. It took a full second for Lund to realize that the thing standing before him was not a gorilla but the animated, half-mechanical corpse of one. One controlled by the living brain inside the jar mounted to a gorilla's neckless corpse. Mechanical orbs for eyes floated in the jar, and carbon microphones for ears sat bolted to the jar's frame.

A struldbrug.

Zuvembies were undying corpses raised up by voodoo. Mindless creations whose decomposed brains were long dead. Struldbrugs, on the other hand, were living brains mounted to dead or dying bodies. Weak individuals fearing death, sought immortality by having their brains pickled in alchemic fluids. Immortal brains in jars fitted back to their aging bodies. And when those died and rotted away, fitted again and again to other corpses or even mechanical replacement bodies. The pain of being so fused to a corpse eventually drove a struldbrug quite insane.

Lund had never seen a gorilla corpse used in a struldbrug, much less one that was half machine. Steel plates covering rotted away flesh, mechanical exoskeletons supplementing shrunken limbs.

The result had driven Gaston Leroux quite mad indeed.

Leroux lashed out with a mechanically-aided gorilla paw, sending the Deseretan end-over-teakettle across the slate tile roof.

Out of the corner of his eye, Lund saw Dupin, drawn to the baton's blue discharge like a bumbling moth to a flame, arrive just in time to receive a second blow that broke ribs and knocked him unconscious, possibly comatose.

Leroux stood on stumpy legs and beat his chest, its mechanical voice roaring in challenge. It then fled, disappearing into the fog.

###

Lund shook his head and wiped the blood trickling down his chin from the corner of his mouth. He managed to activate his springheels in his boot just in time to roll with the blow.

He didn't bother checking on Dupin. Instead, he picked up the fallen baton and jumped after the retreating struldbrug, guided only by the sound of the huge creature's progress and the maps of Paris burned into his brain by the Department's hypnogogic machines.

Not good.

Not only had he and Dupin failed to stop Leroux from slaughtering his last confederate downstairs, but they had failed to capture him once on the roof. And even if Lund did manage to capture the struldbrug, he wasn't sure enough of Leroux's sanity was left to question. The chances for retrieving the mainspring were slim.

The chase led across the rooftops. Leroux with his mechanical eyes could see in the fog much better than Lund. While Lund could leap faster than Leroux could run, several times the fog-blinded Lund misjudged and landed, flailing in the streets below. Once, he crashed through a skylight into an artist's loft, knocking easels and paintings about in the darkened room. Only that fact that

the Leroux's ponderous form could jump across only the narrowest of alleyways kept the rooftop chase on an equal footing.

At last Leroux ran out of rooftops to cross. He teetered on the edge of a warehouse roof, a three-story structure that looked down at the iron rails of a freight line whose tracks cut a swath through the city slum.

Lund landed half a rooftop from the creature, well out of reach of its long gorilla arms. The rod in Lund's hand whined as it built its depleted charge. Almost but not quite. He'd move in when it was ready.

The struldbrug turned and fixed its whirring mechanical eyes upon Lund. "You're no Rue Morgue agent, leaping like a flea as you do." Gears clacked. "Deseretan! One of Sabbas's lapdogs!"

"The mainspring, Leroux. *Now.*"

A mechanical chuckle. "Or what, Mormon? You cannot kill what cannot die."

"Give me what you stole."

"Never!" the horror screeched. "I trade it to be made whole!"

"That's not a promise the ATK can keep. It's been tried."

"ATK!" Leroux sneered. He gestured at his grotesque form. "They did this to me as punishment when that fool of a Rouletabille sent me to infiltrate them! I stole it for *him.* He who can make me whole with it."

"And who is 'him'?"

The monstrous thing twittered, gibbered on insanity's edge. "A ghost, a *fantôme* you can never catch. I go to him now!"

His gorilla legs tensed and he flung himself off the warehouse roof. Down below came the rumble of an incoming freight train, the hiss of its steam engine, the glare of its locomotive headlight cutting through the fog.

So that was Leroux's game. He meant to leap down onto the train and let it carry him away.

A new glow cut through the mist. A jade-green glow that surrounded the falling Leroux, arresting his fall. Pinning him mid-air like a butterfly on a board.

A second glow descended from out of the fog.

The glow-limned figure of a man gently floating in the air. He wore a Hindu turban now, not Astrakhan hat, but Lund recognized him all the same.

The Persian!

The Persian's face was no longer ebony but tanned as a Westerner tans, tanned the shade of his light brown beard. His glowing eyes were just as jade-colored, though.

Power emanated from them. The power of the mind.

He wore an old-fashioned frock coat that draped to the knees. A high-collared European dress shirt with black cravat. Billowing white trousers, creased like western slacks but gathered tightly at the ankle. A patterned Kurdish sash, tied pirate-fashion around his waist and lending Oriental mystery to what was clearly a Caucasian gentleman of means.

"I, Sâr Dubnotal, the Great Psychagogue, the Master of Psychognosis, the Napoleon of the Intangible, know the contents of men's minds!" he thundered as his frame came to rest at eye level with the floating struldbrug three stories above the rumbling train below.

"I know your *fantôme* better than you, monster. He means to use and discard you as you did your own henchmen!"

Leroux struggled against the glow that held him to no avail. "You! He warned me of you!"

"And I'm doing my own warning, Persian," Lund said, drawing his pistol. "You've sold me out once already. I'm not giving you a second chance. The monkey's mine. I need him."

Sâr Dubnotal gestured, and Lund's pistol buried itself back in its holder despite all the strength Lund's wrist and hand used to oppose it. "Patience, my friend."

The floating psychagogue reached over and undid the latches of the collar mechanism attaching brain jar to gorilla corpse.

"*Noooo!*" the jar shouted, a mechanical shout abruptly cancelled in mid-squawk as the cabling unplugged.

Sâr Dubnotal tucked the jar with Leroux's bubbling brain under one arm while with the other removed the green glow around the discarded gorilla corpse. As the glow faded, the rotting body fell three stories to the railbed below.

"Where Rouletabille can find it," Sâr Dubnotal told Lund.

"As for Gaston Leroux himself," the psychagogue patted the jar, "what his master promised with his grand machine, I most assuredly can do with my mind—as I once showed your Mr. Sabbas. I have a private island where I make criminals whole, mind and body. I take Leroux there now."

"Leaving me high and dry," Lund said.

The turbaned man smiled gently. "Did I not say what Leroux knows, I know? This *fantôme* you seek—his name is Erik. Seek him out beneath the stage of the Paris Opera House."

And with that, the psychagogue and his burden flew away into the night.

to be continued in
Part II: A Fright at the Opera

A mysterious Phantom; a long-lost sister;
an underground chase; a trap sprung

With over a hundred professional publication credits, LEE ALLRED's award-winning fiction has appeared in Asimov's Science Fiction, anthologies, magazines, and other venues. He's also scripted for DC (*Batman '66*), Marvel (*Fantastic Four*), IDW (*Dick Tracy*), and Image Comics. Lee's fiction frequently sees print in such Mormon fiction venues as the *Mormon Lit Blitz*, *Wayfare*, *Irreantum*, and anthology publications. He has been nominated numerous times in multiple categories for the Association of Mormon Letters annual awards. "Opera of the Abyss" is set in Lee's Clockwork Deseret series, which has seen multiple installments published in both Mormon and national venues.

KEVIN WASDEN is a fantasy illustrator, writer, and educator whose work combines imaginative world-building with vivid storytelling. He has illustrated for major science fiction and fantasy publishers including Avon Camelot, Baen Books, and Fantasy Flight Games. His portfolio spans book covers, character design, and children's illustration for middle-grade, YA, and adult audiences. Find his work at www.kevinwasden.com.

Essay

Harmony and the Problem of Evil

DC Wynters

*This essay contains spoilers for
the first and second Mistborn series.*

Fantasy is not frivolous. While the genre has often been reduced to formula, fantasy is a means by which authors explore profound questions of the soul. Weronika Łaszkiewicz calls the genre "a modern heir to that mythological tradition in which the fantastic [is] used to question the nature of the material and the spiritual world."*

This modern inheritance is prominently exhibited by Latter-day Saint authors, who often weave religious ideas and themes into their stories. As one example, Latter-day Saint conceptions of humans' ability to become gods appear in as diverse works as Orson Scott Card's *Xenocide*, Stephenie Meyer's *Twilight*, and Charlie Holmberg's *Star Mother*. The prominence of these stories and their religious content in the public imagination is significant for two reasons. First, while Latter-day Saints form a very small minority in the United States, authors from this tradition (such as those named above) are some of the most popular in the science fiction and fantasy genres. These authors have routinely made bestseller lists and, in the case of Brandon Sanderson, have had a

---

* Weronika Łaszkiewicz, *Fantasy Literature and Christianity: A Study of the Mistborn, Coldfire, Fionavar Tapestry and Chronicles of Thomas Covenant Series* (McFarland, 2018), 25.

major impact on the structure of the publishing industry as a whole.

The second reason is more subtle: Many Latter-day Saints are uncomfortable with the idea of everyday members engaging in theology. Theology is defined as "the study of religious faith, practice, and experience."† The topics of theology are generally seen by members of The Church of Jesus Christ of Latter-day Saints as the purview of the Church's leaders, particularly the President of the Church, the First Presidency, and the Quorum of the Twelve Apostles. When members outside of these leadership positions study and write about these topics, it is often seen as an intrusion on the exclusive privilege of those leaders.

This attitude is revealed by Dave Banack's 2013 article "What Mormon Theology Looks Like," where he writes, "the admission that LDS doctrine is firmly in the hands of the Church as an institution and that theology is a largely separate activity makes Mormon theology less threatening."‡ Banack (and Adam S. Miller, whose book is the topic of Banack's article) makes a distinction between doctrine (the official teachings of the Church) and theology as defined above to delineate the territory where everyday members may operate. In this framework, a Latter-day Saint has no ability to change the official teachings while still being able to engage in theology. Such a distinction is necessary because of Church members' deep respect for prophetic/institutional authority and the widespread assumption that said authority has exclusive claim to theological matters.

Despite this hesitance among some, the literature of the Latter-day Saints is full of theology. Fantasy provides a context in which Latter-day Saints can engage in discussions that might otherwise be seen as suspect or subversive. Fantasy worlds, whether secondary or not, provide a sandbox where authors can reason about God, faith, and religion without direct application to our own reality. Sometimes,

---

† "Theology," *Merriam-Webster.com Dictionary*.
‡ Dave Banack, "What Mormon Theology Looks Like," *Times & Seasons*, January 15, 2013, https://archive.timesandseasons.org/2013/01/what-mormon-theology-looks-like/index.html

these theological experiments lead to different conclusions than those taught by the institutional church

As an initial example of this thesis, I examine the theological content of Brandon Sanderson's *Wax & Wayne* series. Weronika Łaskiewicz reviewed the series as a whole in her book *Fantasy Literature and Christianity*. In contrast, I focus on one theological theme in the series: the problem of evil. Sanderson addresses this perennial Christian problem in a series of dialogues between the main character of the series, Wax, and the god called Harmony. These dialogues not only incorporate elements of Latter-day Saint solutions to the problem of evil, but also move beyond them to engage in meaningful dialogue with the broader religious community.

Introduction to the Problem of Evil

One of the clearest formulations of the problem of evil was put forward by David L. Paulsen in his address "Joseph Smith and the Problem of Evil."* This problem of evil is based on three propositions, any two of which require that the third be false. The propositions are as follows:

1. God is omnipotent.
2. God is all-loving.
3. Evil exists.

The first two propositions are core claims about the nature of God in Christianity, Islam, and Judaism, while the third is an incontrovertible fact of life. Theologians have spilled much ink working through this problem, and many traditions contain theodicies (or answers to the problem of evil) within their scriptures. In the Latter-day Saint tradition, one of the most prominent theodicies is a revelation recorded by Joseph Smith in 1839 while imprisoned in Liberty, Missouri. This revelation now forms sections 121, 122, and 123 of the Doctrine and Covenants.

For the purposes of this essay, these sections of the Doctrine and Covenants will serve as a launching-off point for a broader comparison between current Latter-day Saint theodicies and the theodicy contained in the *Wax & Wayne* series. First, I will examine the similarities and

---

* David L. Paulsen, "Joseph Smith and the Problem of Evil," *BYU Forum*, 1999, https://speeches.byu.edu/talks/david-l-paulsen/joseph-smith-problem-evil/.

the differences between these two texts. This examination will reveal both the theological content of the *Wax & Wayne* series and Sanderson's dialogue with the broader Christian community. Then, I will consider how these texts treat the existence of evil. I will conclude with an assessment of how Sanderson's Harmony has more in common with modern progressive Christian conceptions of God than those currently emphasized by the institution of the Church.

Similarities

Scholars of religion use Rudolf Otto's concept of the numinous to understand the ways in which religious texts and rituals are experienced. Łaszkiewicz describes Otto's numinous as "an inexplicable and unattainable entity which frightens people and fascinates them at the same time"† and outlines four categories for the experience of the numinous. The last of these categories, the *mysterium tremendum,* is an overwhelming sense of the majesty and incomprehensibility of God. Łaszkiewicz describes it as the simultaneous sense of smallness of self and the grandness of the divine, often characterized by awe and terror.

The *mysterium tremendum* appears in both Joseph's revelation and the *Wax & Wayne* series. In the former, the *mysterium tremendum* is centered on God's infinite suffering. After an extensive list of tribulations that Joseph may be called to suffer, the Lord says, "The Son of Man hath descended below them all. Art thou greater than he?" (D&C 122:8). God's suffering, Joseph's revelation explains, exceeds mortal imagination. In an earlier revelation, the immensity of this suffering is described as being so immense that it "caused myself, even God, the greatest of all, to tremble because of pain, and to bleed at every pore, and to suffer both body and spirit" (D&C 19:18). In the context of Liberty Jail, these descriptions of God's suffering would have served to diminish Joseph and his coreligionists' mortal suffering while emphasizing the horror and majesty of God's suffering.

In the *Wax & Wayne* series, the *mysterium tremendum* centers on Harmony's inscrutability. When Wax interrogates Harmony on why he does not intervene to prevent more suffering, Harmony replies, "Should I prevent all hardship, Waxillium? [...] And once nobody is ever hurt, [...] will people be satisfied?"‡ Harmony's reasoning is similar to a slippery slope argument. Because the inhabitants of Scadrial will be dissatisfied in some way regardless of the presence of suffering, the decision of how much

---

† Łaskiewicz, *Fantasy Literature and Christianity,* 34.
‡ Brandon Sanderson, *The Bands of Mourning* (Tor, 2016), 450.

suffering to allow must be based on some other factor. While the logic is perfectly comprehensible, Harmony's decision of where to draw the line is beyond reproach due to the radical imbalance of power between himself and Wax. While Wax does protest that Harmony should do more to prevent suffering, Harmony is unmoved. This *mysterium tremendum* is more in line with that evoked by the biblical story of God's commandment to Abraham to sacrifice his son Isaac. In both stories, God's impunity emphasizes the smallness of humanity and the terrible might of divinity.

While both stories exhibit the *mysterium tremendum*, the difference in objects used to inspire the phenomenon demonstrates the difference in intended audience between the two texts. Joseph's revelation is addressed to his coreligionists and so operates based off shared understanding of both Joseph's earlier revelations and the Christian teaching (emphasized

> ## "Should I prevent all hardship, Waxillium? And once nobody is ever hurt, will people be satisfied?"

in the Latter-day Saint tradition) that Jesus bore the weight of infinite suffering in His crucifixion. The *Wax & Wayne* series is, by contrast, addressed to a popular audience where a shared religious understanding cannot be assumed. Harmony's inscrutability reflects the universal human experience of encountering the absurdity of life. Indeed, the presence of evil in the world is one of the most obvious catalysts for this feeling. Many people, when seeking causes for suffering, are met with the universe's silence, much in the same way that Wax is met with Harmony's inscrutability in their dialogue. Thus, Sanderson engages those outside of the Latter-day Saint community with an experience of the *mysterium tremendum* that is universally understandable.

The second commonality between the two texts is an emphasis on God's compassion and emotional capacity. Both Joseph's God and Harmony promise to be with the sufferer. In Joseph's revelation, the Lord promises to "stand by [him] forever" (D&C 122:4). The Lord's commitment to Joseph recalls a passage from the book of Moses in the Pearl of Great Price and one of the most striking images of God in the Latter-day Saint tradition. In this earlier revelation, the prophet Enoch is lifted up to behold creation and witnesses God weeping for the evil in the world (Moses 7). These two revelations, taken together, describe a God who suffers with His children and weeps with them.

Harmony goes further and says that he "[loathes] suffering."* In both cases, the image of God runs counter to that displayed in classical Christian theology. Broader Christianity, drawing upon ancient Greek conceptions of perfection, asserts that God is unchangeable and therefore does not have emotions. The reasoning goes that because emotions are reactions to circumstance and God cannot be changed by circumstance, God cannot feel emotions. Compassion is still attributed to God in this case, but compassion is understood as persistent care for creation rather than an emotional reaction. In contrast, both Joseph and Sanderson insist on a God whose love is made manifest through emotional responses to the suffering of His creatures, whether that emotional response be sorrow or loathing. In Sanderson's case, presenting the image of a God who has emotional responses to creation is an offering of a Latter-day Saint idea to his audience.

Differences

For all their commonalities, there are significant differences between the two texts. To begin, the two deities have different goals in their responses to evil. In D&C 121, the Lord promises to destroy those responsible for the persecution of the Saints, exemplifying a common image of God in eighteenth and nineteenth-century America as an avenger. The imagery that Smith uses to describe the Lord's forthcoming vengeance emphasizes the greatness of His power in comparison to the wicked. For example, the Lord says of the wicked that "their hope shall be blasted, and their prospects shall melt away as the hoar frost melteth before the burning rays of the rising sun" (D&C 121:11). The second image in particular uses the difference between an astronomical object and ephemeral frost to convey God's grandeur.

By contrast, when Harmony dispatches Wax to kill Bleeder, he couches his goals in the language of harm reduction: "I hate that Bleeder must be allowed to do what they do. I cannot stop them. You can. I beg

---

* Brandon Sanderson, *Shadows of Self* (Tor, 2015), 146.

you to do so."* Harmony never tells Wax that he is punishing Bleeder, rather he emphasizes concern for how Bleeder's activities may hurt the other inhabitants of Scadrial. Sanderson thus avoids the image of the wrathful God in Joseph's revelation, instead offering a God exhibiting universal concern. For a broader society that prizes equality, Harmony's desire to prevent harm is more attractive than a God who punishes those who antagonize His chosen people.

Another difference can be seen in the relationship between the deities and their addressees. In D&C 121, the Lord calls Joseph His son. While this does reflect the unique Latter-day Saint belief that humans are literal spirit children of God, it also serves to link Joseph's suffering with Jesus's suffering. This is one of the ways that suffering is given its redemptive quality in the Latter-day Saint tradition, a point to which I will return later in this essay.

Harmony never addresses Wax as his son, and it is well known that Harmony is not the literal spiritual father of humanity. As such, Harmony's decision about how to relate to mortals is made outside of the context of parenthood. Furthermore, Harmony has replaced an actively malevolent deity. Harmony choosing to protect and care for the inhabitants of Scadrial is a way he seeks to be a more worthy god than the Lord Ruler.

The final difference is in the level of power each of these deities possesses. Harmony makes it clear to Wax that he is not omnipotent when he says, "My hands are tied, and I am bounded."† This in contrast to the assumed omnipotence attributed to the Latter-day Saint God in D&C 121. I say assumed because the descriptions of God's impending justice, both in its inescapability and in its might, are consistent with an omnipotent God. However, the Book of Mormon describes God as being bound by a law of justice and a law of mercy (Alma 42). In a similar vein, Harmony says, "I hold both Ruin and Preservation [...] I

---

* Sanderson, *Shadows*, 146.
† Sanderson, *Shadows*, 145.

am balance. And, to an extent, I am neutrality." ‡The fact that both deities are limited by principles means that the difference in power between the two gods is a soft difference.

The Redemption of Suffering

With an understanding of the theological similarities and differences between the two texts, I now turn to consider how each text attempts to reconcile the existence of evil with God's attributes. While some theologians focus on how the attributes of God's omnipotence or loving kindness can be defined in such a way as to make them consistent with evil, these two texts focus on the attributes of evil and how they may be made consistent with God's character. In so doing, they attempt to "redeem" suffering, or to define evil in such a way that the problem of evil can be resolved.

The broader Christian tradition in which Joseph was operating sometimes conceptualized suffering as a means by which God makes humanity holy (or, in other words, sanctifies humanity). This idea is present in D&C 121 when the Lord says, "if thou endure it well, God shall exalt thee on high" (D&C 121:8) and "all these things shall give thee experience, and shall be for thy good" (D&C 122:7). However, the redemption of

suffering operates on two additional levels in this revelation.

First, God's power is manifested by vengeance at the Final Judgment. While evil may not be recompensed immediately, or even in a mortal lifetime, God promises to right the scales of justice by punishing the wicked. Thus, no evil goes unpunished and God's power is preserved.

Second, God's love is manifested by Jesus's suffering. In the words of the Book of Mormon, God "offereth himself a sacrifice for sin" (2 Nephi 2:7) and has partaken of and borne the weight of all possible evil (Alma 7:11). This conceptualization of Jesus's suffering is reenacted in the Latter-day Saint sacrament ordinance. Through the sacrament, Jesus's suffering is lifted out of time to take place here and now, thus providing a ritual reminder that God will suffer and weep with His children as Joseph's revelations explain. Thus, suffering is redeemed as it occurs, rather than only at the Final Judgment.

In contrast, Harmony never claims that the existence of suffering is necessary for individual improvement. He does say that struggle prompts technological advancement: "You were to have had the radio a century ago, but you didn't need it, so you didn't strive for it."§ In this formulation, impersonal, societal evil is seen as

---

‡ Sanderson, *Shadows*, 145.

§ Sanderson, *Shadows*, 146.

having the potential to "redeem" groups of people by pushing for technological advancement, but individual suffering is seen as something to be prevented.

Harmony also does not promise to avenge all wrongdoing in the future. It appears that Harmony either has no desire to do so or his powers are not sufficient.

Finally, Harmony's redemption of evil is not ritualized in the same way as it is in the Latter-day Saint tradition. Harmony's system of worship does not have any recognizable rituals

Conclusions

It is clear that the *Wax & Wayne* series draws deeply on Latter-day Saint ideas to explore the problem of evil. However, Sanderson emphasizes different aspects of God's relationship to suffering than those currently emphasized by Latter-day Saint leaders.

Contemporary Church leaders emphasize the teaching that suffering is redeemed at the Final Judgment when God punishes the wicked and rewards the faithful. This doctrine, shared with broader Christianity

> **Harmony's redemption of evil is the same as the redemption represented in the sacrament: he, like Jesus, witnesses the evil of the world and suffers with humanity.**

outside of meditation, and hence Harmony's followers lack a ritual language for the redemption of evil.

That is not to say that Harmony does not redeem evil. Indeed, Harmony's redemption of evil is the same as the redemption represented in the sacrament: he, like Jesus, witnesses the evil of the world and suffers with humanity. It is the heavenly presence in suffering, extended out of pure love, that constitutes the ultimate redemption of evil for both texts.

and solidly based in the revelations that I have considered here, couches the sanctification of suffering in forward-looking expectation. The *Wax & Wayne* series emphasizes a God who suffers with humanity in the present. In this view, suffering is not redeemed by a future righting of the balances, but rather is redeemed by God passing through affliction with His children. This idea has a lesser reliance on the Final Judgment and a greater reliance on a God who is ever present and active. As before, this doctrine is solidly based in the revelations considered in this essay and is shared with broader Christianity. These differing emphases are not a contradiction; they are two faces of the jewel that is the Latter-day Saint faith.

That being said, Harmony's characterization is more in line with Thomas Jay Oord's theory of God's power than the omnipotence of traditional monotheism. Oord uses the word amipotence to describe God's power, and which can be defined by three attributes:

1. Amipotence is limited.
2. Amipotence is motivated by love.
3. Amipotence requires the cooperation of mortal agents.*

Harmony clearly exhibits these characteristics. As explained above, Harmony has limited power and is motivated by love. The last point, that an amipotent God requires the cooperation of mortal agents, is shown by Harmony's final explanation of the problem of evil in *The Bands of Mourning*: "When I hold back, staying my hand from protecting those below, [...] I must do it out of trust in what people can do on their own."†

The figure of Harmony demonstrates how one Latter-day Saint author uses fantasy to engage in theological meditations about God's nature and His relationship to suffering. The close concordance with Oord's amipotent God is an example of how these theological experiments can lead to surprising and fruitful dialogue with other religious traditions. I hope that future Latter-day Saint authors follow Sanderson's example and use the fantasy genre to engage in theology. May we all benefit from their surprising and delightful experiments.

---

* Thomas Jay Oord, *The Death of Omnipotence and Birth of Amipotence* (SacraSage, 2023).

† Sanderson, *Bands*, 452.

DC WYNTERS is a fantasy and science fiction author from the Pacific Northwest and a cohost on the writing podcast *Quid Prose Quo*. He is the author of *The Shadowrunner*, *The Black Crescent*, and "The Archaemaji." He and his wife are music leaders in their ward. Subscribe to his newsletter at dcwynters.substack.com for updates on his upcoming projects.

Poetry

Ivy
Sadie Marie Hutchings

I knew a girl born with ivy
in a ring around her wrist.
Every few years it grew.
The tender
jealous leaves crept up her forearm,
her collar,
her throat. She named it Guilt
and meant by that:
all the things she had ever done wrong.

Its foliage, a heavy emerald bracelet
and necklace; a choking weight:
verdant and lush as she aged.

We met again this past November
and I was surprised to see
the pale white
of her neck and arms exposed. No
trace of chlorophyll, no
climbing vines.

She laughed and made a joke
that she'd finally tan.
She told me, self-forgiveness: the hatchet.
God's grace, the strong arm swinging.

SADIE MARIE HUTCHINGS is a poet and artist living in the Salt Lake City area. Her poetry and prose have been published in *Exponent II*, as well as Emerson College's *Stork* and *Generic* literary magazines. A reader as much as a writer, Sadie Marie is currently most excited about the launch of *Still Small Stories*, a weekly Substack publication of short fiction of which she is a founding editor.

Fiction

COMMITMENT

BRIAN K. LOWE

I FOUND THE ARCHANGEL GABRIEL sitting on a bench in the park.

He was just resting there, his horn sitting in his lap as though he'd been playing for the quarters passers-by would drop in his hat, overturned on the sidewalk at his feet. The nearest street lamp was burned out, but in the glow from the lamp down the path a ways, I could see that his coat was worn and his trousers were shiny at the knees.

It was impossible to tell how old he might be. But of course he wasn't just some old Black musician, down on his luck and years removed from his days with Benny Goodman—he was the archangel Gabriel, and he was sitting on my bench.

I lowered myself onto the wet wood next to him, my bones cracking and snapping like a breakfast cereal commercial. Nobody was walking by for him to play for. It was long past midnight, much closer to dawn than it appeared to the naked eye. Dew had started to settle on the ground and the sleeping statues. But if he didn't mind the solitude and the wet bench, why then, I didn't either. At least those things I had been expecting. Gabriel didn't speak when I sat down, nor move nor raise his head, either.

Even so late—or so early, depending on how you reckon time—I could hear the murmur of cars on the boulevard, out of sight behind the big old dying elm trees. A long time ago I stopped wondering why business kept people out at such hours, including me. It was our pact; I didn't ask them and they didn't ask me.

"You know who I am," he said at last. It was a question without a question mark. He knew I knew; he just needed me to know I could trust myself.

"Yes," I said, nodding a bit, though he hadn't looked at me. "I recognized you. When I was a boy, my mother was always looking for the Truth, even though she didn't have any idea where to find it. One Sunday she dragged me to a Baptist church downtown. We were the only white people there. Even the figures in the murals and paintings were Black. I've never forgotten that. On the wall directly opposite our pew was a painting of Gabriel appearing before the Virgin Mary. He had your face."

His head was still back on the bench, watching Heaven.

"Do you believe it?"

"I'm sorry?"

"You know who I am, but do you believe it?"

I thought he must be playing with me. "Isn't that the same thing?"

"No." He wasn't arguing with me, more like resigned to letting me have my point of view. "Do you know why I'm here?" he asked abruptly.

"No," I admitted.

He opened his eyes and looked straight ahead. "It's time."

"Oh." There was a little flutter in my stomach—I would have thought it would be my heart, but no matter. I pulled in a deep breath of cold morning, looked around at the elms that were going to outlast me after all, straightened my frayed cuffs, and looked at him. "All right then. Let's go."

Gabriel smiled sadly at the sky. "No, not for you, Arthur. For everything."

Well, that was unexpected. The flutter in my stomach went away, replaced by curiosity, and maybe a bit of excitement—the kind of guilty excitement you feel when you think maybe there's going to be a fight.

Ill: *isaxar/Shutterstock.com*

"Really?" I felt like a kid again, that Christmas when I saw a big present under the tree and it had my name on it.

Gabriel nodded at last. "Really."

"You don't look very happy about it." In the dark, I heard the material of his jacket move as he shrugged.

"It gets old after a while."

I frowned. "You've done this before?"

He sighed. "About a thousand times. Whenever it's necessary. It's not for the whole universe, just for you folks, but it happens to everyone eventually."

"Everyone? You mean—?"

"Yes," he said.

My eyes got wide. I looked up, as he was doing, but instead of heaven I saw the billions of other lives I'd always dreamed about, revolving around thousands of other suns, the lives described by Burroughs and Heinlein and Asimov. "It's a shame you never got to meet any of the others."

I was thrown back to Earth. "Would it have helped?"

His voice was very soft. "No."

My dreams dashed, we fell into silence again. The street murmurs had grown almost imperceptibly louder, but not so much as to break the spell. The day was approaching.

I was fearful to rouse him, afraid to hasten whatever terrible calamity the rage of heaven might take, but his silence was an invitation, engraved on the air.

"So why me? Why my bench?"

He sighed with palpable relief. "Because I only carry the horn; I don't blow it. That has to be one of wyou. It's the last test of free will."

"But why me? I haven't been to church in years."

"But I believe you still have faith. As tattered and fragile as it is, you still believe."

That was news to me. "I'm afraid I stopped believing in anything besides this bench a long time ago." I thought about that big present, and the morning I unwrapped it to find it was only a much smaller toy my parents had stuffed in a big box to fool me. "I don't know if I believe in God any more. I used to, but now I'm just kind of an agnostic."

Gabriel chuckled almost silently. "No you're not, Arthur. An agnostic is nothing but an atheist with a fear of commitment. Maybe you haven't been to church in seventeen years, but you're a good man; in many ways, you're the most honest man on Earth. In the ways that count, Arthur," he said quickly, as if he knew my objection. "In the ways that only you and I can see. You never betrayed yourself. Besides," he added with more warmth, "you play." He indicated the trumpet in his lap. "Anybody *could* play it—but it sounds best when it's in the hands of a man who knows how. I think your world deserves that."

"What happens if I play it?"

"The world ends."

That was when I realized he was crazy. I don't know why I hadn't realized it before; maybe I wasn't cut out for these late nights anymore. He wasn't an archangel any more than I was the reincarnation of Britain's greatest king. He thought I could play, and I hadn't played since the day I realized that no matter how long I practiced, I'd never be in a real orchestra, never be anything more than third trumpet in a mediocre high school band. I'd had faith in that dream, knew if I worked hard enough I could make it someday—and it never happened. Just like I never became a great lawyer, never more than a one-man personal injury office. That was where my faith had gone. It had faded with my dreams.

And the last of all, held with white-knuckled intensity, had been the one dream I'd thought life couldn't take away. After all, you can't really know if you were right about God until you're dead, and then it's a little late to worry about whether you were wrong. But I had been wrong, when I thought there was a dream, a hope, that life couldn't extinguish. I had

counted on logic to sustain hope, but I had not counted on how long a life can be, how many disappointments one can be asked to endure.

But here He was. Not God Himself, but as close as you could ask for. Or so said some out-of-work musician who couldn't afford a flophouse.

"Arthur," Gabriel said with soft urgency, and I realized only then that I'd gotten to my feet. "I picked you for this because you still aren't lost. You still want to believe. But if you walk away from me now, you won't have another chance. Someone else will blow it, someone who may not have your faith."

"What do you mean? What difference does it make? The world is going to end. You said so yourself." I was beginning to doubt myself. What was I doing, talking to some stranger in the park at five in the morning?

"It makes a great deal of difference, Arthur. It literally makes all the difference in the world. If you blow the horn out of faith—faith that something more awaits, something that you cannot see—then something better will come. But if he who blows the horn does it simply because he has been bidden, without any belief in something outside of himself, then the world just ends.

There is no more. All of human history will count for nothing."

His "last act of free will" was my last act of faith. "But I can't do that. I can't take on the responsibility for all mankind. I don't know what to do. If only I had some proof—"

"No proof, Arthur. Proof is the death of faith. That is why I asked you—you *know* me, but do you *believe* me?"

I wanted Gabriel's story to be true, to be proof that what I believed was right. But how could I prove myself right, when the mere act of proving it made me wrong?

The first gray was coming on in the east. Time waits for no man. I could see the trumpet a little better now.

I had to admit, it looked like a very fine instrument.

Originally published in Age of Certainty *(2013).*

BRIAN K. LOWE lives on the outskirts of Los Angeles with his wife and a host of voices in his head clamoring to be heard. He is a member of SFWA, and his thoughts and writings can be found at brianklowe.wordpress.com.

Fiction

THE DOUBLE-SNATCHER

WO HEMSATH

THE DAYLIGHT CLAWING DOWN through the branches was slowly dying. In its place, a growing breeze scraped through the trees, too cold for this time of year.

Aasim Beaver sat on his haunches, his wide tail tapping the ground. This new wind didn't carry the smell of cedars or date palms. It smelled of danger and darkness.

It smelled of death.

His tail tapped faster. They should all be in their homes, preparing for whatever was coming. Not gathered like fools discussing the health of local mushroom colonies or squabbling over territories. But Nahar loved these little gatherings, and now that she was pregnant, he wouldn't let her come alone. He would protect his family at all costs.

He could not fail again.

Nahar rested her tail gently, but firmly, atop his to still it and urged his gaze back to the gnarled stump in the center of the crowd of animals. A wizened brown hare with a half-severed ear ended his rant with a thump of his hind leg, then hopped off the stump.

A mongoose—this season's community chair-mammal, according to Nahar—scurried atop the stump in his place.

"Thank you," she squeaked, "for that important reminder that scent markers make good neighbors. Remember to mark what's yours and respect what's not." A tendril of icy air rushed past her, and she shivered. "If there's no further business—"

"What of my parents?" a deep voice asked from beyond the circle of gathered creatures. Two sharp, ridged horns pierced the lengthening shadows as an adolescent gazelle stepped forward.

"That's the boy I told you about," Nahar whispered to Aasim. "He called on the council last week for help finding his parents. They disappeared one night and haven't returned. He's busy caring for his younger sisters, poor dear. Otherwise he'd go looking himself."

The mongoose wouldn't meet the gazelle's eyes. "Yes, um . . . you see . . . ."

"Won't be no search," the wizened hare grumbled. All ears flicked toward him. The mongoose shot him a disapproving look which he met with a defiant thump.

"Boy's grown. He don't need hoof holdin'. He needs the truth." He turned to the gazelle. "Wolves got your folks. That's the sorry truth. Makes no sense riskin' our lives to look for bones. It's best you move on."

The gazelle reared and struck his hooves into the forest floor as his voice charged through the night. "It wasn't wolves!"

Aasim grabbed Nahar's paw to pull her away. He wouldn't risk her being around if a fight broke out.

Directly overhead, a branch snapped. Every creature stilled, eyes and ears searching, assessing.

More branches shuddered, drawing closer. Aasim tugged at Nahar, but she resisted and pointed at a giant heron hopping down towards the clearing. "It's only Traveler."

Nahar often mentioned the news-bringing bird, claiming he was harmless. Aasim didn't trust outsiders, however. Especially those with snake-like necks and beaks as sharp as human spears.

The heron perched on the lowest branch, looming over them. "The boy is right. Wolves are not behind these disappearances."

Ill: George S. Harris & Sons, Beaver, from the Wild Animals of the World series (1888), The Metropolitan Museum of Art, New York

"These?" The mongoose quivered atop the stump. "There have been more?"

Traveler bobbed his head. "Two water buffalo a day's flight from here, brother and sister. And a pair of owls, too. There's never blood, no sign of struggle, no saying good-bye."

"What happened to them?" the gazelle asked.

"Not what. Who." The heron leapt from his branch to the center of their gathering and lowered his voice. "The Double-Snatcher."

All the animals cowered slightly. The heron stalked his way around his audience on spindly legs, wings spreading dramatically as he spoke.

"He doesn't hunt. He doesn't trap. He doesn't use anything except . . . magic!" A stick shot up, clutched in his talons. Those closest to him flinched. He smiled as he tucked the thin branch under his wing and continued prowling. "His staff has the power to snatch control of your very mind. Under his spell, you'll leave all that you love to slither, walk, or fly straight to him. And what does he do once you arrive?"

Not even Aasim breathed during the suspended silence.

"He feeds you to a ravenous beast!" The heron snapped his beak at an unsuspecting hedgehog and reveled in the resulting squeaks and startled squeals. "In all my travels, I've never seen its likeness. A true leviathan of the land that could cross your river in a single stride." Nahar huddled closer to Aasim as the heron continued. "It crouches on its many legs outside a human colony, demanding to be fed. Beneath its row of unnatural eyes is a gaping mouth that never shuts. The beast swallows animals whole and doesn't bother spitting out the bones."

Beside Aasim, Nahar trembled. The last of the sunlight drained from the forest, and the heron's beady eyes glinted in the shadowy night. This bird clearly enjoyed the power his stories had, and Aasim was done letting Nahar be terrorized by

Ill: George S. Harris & Sons, Persian Gazelle, from the Wild Animals of the World series (1888), The Metropolitan Museum of Art, New York

them. He pulled her away, and she came without protest.

As they headed for the river, she crept beside him, searching the shadows on either side of their path.

"It was only a full-moon tale," he assured her. "The kind you tell young kits so they'll stay close to the lodge. There is no mind-snatching man."

"But Traveler saw him."

"Traveler saw a gullible audience. He's a performer. Don't let him get under your fur."

"The gazelles did disappear though. And there wasn't any blood."

"No blood where they were last seen," he corrected. "They wandered from the safety of their home, and I'm sure wherever they were caught, there were signs of wolves or humans." He eyed her seriously. "Regular, non-magic humans that our lodge protects us from."

They emerged from the meager shelter of the trees, and the icy wind raked across them unrestrained. It clawed the normally smooth surface of their dammed-off pond, disfiguring the reflected face of the full-moon into a ragged skull.

Aasim shivered. The wind would only get stronger as the night wore on. The Double-Snatcher might not be real, but the danger of this storm was.

Nahar paused at the water's edge. Her paws fretted over each other. Aasim stilled them with his own and raised his voice to be heard over the

"Beneath its row of unnatural eyes is a gaping mouth that never shuts. The beast swallows animals whole and doesn't bother spitting out the bones."

rising gusts. "I will keep you safe." He stared meaningfully at her belly. "All of you."

She nodded, then slid into the pond, letting its inky waters consume her.

Aasim followed her down to the watery entrance and up into the tunnel that led to the dry chambers of their lodge. They'd come home just in time. Beyond the vent hole at the top of their main chamber, the wind rushed faster and faster as if trying to escape something close on its heels.

Outside, wind-whipped debris pelted the wood and mud walls of their lodge. "They'll hold," Aasim said, nestling beside Nahar.

He reassured himself of everything he'd done to make this new lodge thicker and stronger than their last, yet this wind was like none he'd ever seen. It gnashed and tore at their roof. Chunks of mud ripped free around the vent hole, and the tightly woven sticks across the opening began to rattle. Nahar buried her head against him, whimpering.

The wind howled, vicious and hungry, devouring pieces of their home above them. All Aasim could do was hold Nahar and fight back memories of teeth and growls and other howls—of frantic cries and blood-stained dirt and scattered tufts of newborn fur.

The wind attacked for hours. When it left, their roof bore a gaping wound, and the vast uncertainty of the night bled in. Thick clouds now dammed the once moonlit sky.

Aasim sniffed tentatively. The air was heavy with the smell of coming rain. "We won't have long to make repairs. A day or two at most. I need to get started."

"Now?" Nahar followed him to the exit tunnel. "It's too dark. You haven't slept."

"I'll sleep once I know the lodge is fixed and you'll be safe."

"Let me help."

Aasim rested his paw on her swollen belly. "The kits need you to rest. The sun will rise in a few hours, and I'll have worked up an appetite by then. I'll come home, and we'll eat together."

"I could make cattail soup," she offered.

"I don't want you leaving the lodge." He motioned to their stockpile of tubers. "We have plenty to eat already."

The water level in the exit tunnel looked lower than before; their pond was slowly draining. Part of the dam must have been weakened as well. That would have to be his first repair.

"If I'm not back by breakfast, I will be by midday," he said. "No matter what, promise me you won't leave the lodge?"

She nodded, and he slid into the watery black.

Aasim had been right about the dam; the wind had left a bite in it, and the draining water was slowly eroding and enlarging the hole. He patched it easily enough with mud and branches, careful not to thump too loudly—Nahar needed her rest.

Repairs weren't enough, though. If the clouds overhead proved as vicious as the wind that brought them, the rain might raise the river. He needed to make their dam taller, stronger. He had to keep Nahar safe.

Aasim made his way into the forest, the branches overhead nothing more than dark scratches against an already black world. He moved as quietly as he could, straining in the dark for the right size tree.

He found one that might work, and paced around it. It was thicker than he needed but perhaps he could use it to reinforce—

To his right, the underbrush rustled. Aasim froze, fur bristled. His heart thumped louder than his tail ever had, but he couldn't see anything. Nothing smelled out of place.

When nothing attacked, Aasim began gnawing the tree. He ignored the prickling at the base of his fur every time he heard the forest shift. If he was going to reinforce the whole length of the dam and make it even higher, he would need a lot of trees. He didn't have time to waste on fear.

The sun had been trapped behind the wall of clouds for hours before Aasim patted the last bit of mud atop the fortified dam. He'd spent all night and morning felling trees, floating them downriver, and fixing them in place. Thankfully, Nahar had slept through it all. He couldn't let her sleep any longer though.

"I've stabilized the pond," he called from atop his massive dam. "I'll gather the branches to fix the roof if you want to start preparing the tubers. I'll do the repairs after we eat."

Only the rushing of the river replied.

His voice should have carried through the torn roof. She should have heard him, even in the sleeping chamber. Fear gnawed his belly, but he shook it off like water. They'd had a traumatic night. Nahar was probably too deeply asleep.

Aasim walked across the top of the dam to the riverbank. She was fine. She'd promised to stay in the lodge, and there'd been no signs of predators. If she was still sleeping, he should let her keep sleeping.

And he would. After he checked on her.

He dove into the pond and swam up the tunnel to the main chamber, now flooded with the dim gray of day. He wouldn't even have to wake her. One quick peek to make sure she was fine, and then he'd—

The sleeping chamber was empty.

"Nahar?"

He checked the back tunnel and rechecked the main chamber and sleeping chamber.

Empty.

Empty.

Empty.

He scurried down the tunnel and back onto shore. "Nahar!"

He called her over and over, louder and longer until his voice was raw.

She never called back.

He ran downriver toward the cattails. Maybe she'd gone to gather ingredients, even though he'd told her not too.

The cattails were empty, though. Deep down, he'd known they would be. Something as simple as soup would never make Nahar break her promise.

But the Double-Snatcher might.

The thought snaked its way into his mind, and he tried to fight it back. There had to be a logical explanation. Magic and mind-snatching weren't real. The Double-Snatcher couldn't be real. Even if he was, he took creatures two at a time. Nahar had been alone.

Aasim followed the river downstream, sniffing for clues and calling her name. Impossibly, the wall of clouds in the sky thickened and darkened with more and more clouds until it seemed it would burst. Aasim reached the scent mound marking the end of their territory without so much as a trace of her. However, he hadn't caught scent of a predator either. That was good. She was probably upriver somewhere. He'd cross to the other bank and work his way toward their upper boundary.

He was halfway across the river when a wail rose above the water's rumbling. The cry was farther downstream, but there was no mistaking it—a beaver was in distress.

He launched himself downstream, swimming with the current as fast as he could, ignoring his neighbor's scent mounds as he entered their territory. The cries and moans grew louder, separating into two distinct voices. Neither were Nahar's.

Around the bend, an impressive lodge rose into view. It had fared the storm better than his own.

"Berosh!" a male beaver called above the distraught wails of the female beside him. "Berosh!"

Aasim exited the river just above their pond. The male stepped protectively in front of the female, slapped his broad tail on the water, and bared his sharp, orange incisors.

"I don't mean to trespass." Aasim kept himself at a safe distance, front paws in the air. "I heard crying."

"Our son." The female stifled her sobs. "We were all sleeping in the lodge, but when we woke this morning, he was gone. It's been hours."

"He's two," the father said reluctantly. "It is possible he went searching for a wife and place of his own."

His wife slapped her tail atop his. "You know he'd never leave without saying good-bye!"

Aasim steadied himself on all fours as the earth started to spin around him like a whirlpool. Two beavers mysteriously gone. No signs of blood.

"Have you seen or heard anything?" the mother asked.

"No." Aasim's voice came out as weak as his limbs. "My wife . . ."

"She saw something?"

He shook his head. "She's missing too."

The mother wailed anew—a loud, soul-scraping sound—and the urge to join her nearly consumed Aasim. But either Nahar was fine, or she needed his help. Either way, crying wouldn't do any good. He met the father's eyes. "I'll keep an eye out for your son."

The father nodded with a look that promised to do the same for

Nahar, but there was no hope in his eyes, only the familiar sorrow of a father now childless—a sorrow Aasim wasn't ready to face again.

Nahar and their unborn kits had to be okay.

He had to keep hoping.

He had to find Traveler.

###

She'll be dead before you get there.

That's what the heron had said—once his laughter died—when Aasim asked where to find the Double-Snatcher. He'd finally given Aasim directions though.

A day's flight with the sun to your left.

Aasim didn't know how many days of walking equaled one day of flying, but so far it was more than five—if he was going in the right direction. It was hard to keep something on your left that you couldn't even see. Gray clouds smothered the world around him. They should have burst days ago but continued to darken. The air was heavy enough to drown in. Beneath him, the earth was hard and cracked with only a few stubborn shrubs daring to grow amongst the dirt and rocks.

By the time he'd found the heron and gotten directions, Nahar had already been gone half a day. He'd run for hours, hoping to catch up. Running became walking. Walking became dragging. At times he thought

he caught her scent—the increased humidity should have made it easy. But it was so faint and fleeting, he couldn't be sure he hadn't imagined it. Now his legs threatened to collapse like chewed trees, and he stopped to rest again.

The further from the lodge he trekked, the more foolish he felt. Did he really believe a magic human had snatched control of Nahar's mind? What if she'd only wandered to the other side of the forest, perhaps to help those orphaned gazelles? What if she came home to find him gone?

Aasim had done his best to avoid any sign of animal life for fear of predators, but if the Double-Snatcher was real and anywhere nearby, the animals of the area would surely know.

She'll be dead before you get there.

In the distance, the tops of hills peeked over the horizon. If he pushed himself, he could get there in a few hours. The elevated view would help him scout out an area most likely to have local animal life, and if whoever he found hadn't heard of the Double-Snatcher, he'd go home.

The idea to turn back ate at him as he dragged himself forward, but what else could he do? He would give his life for Nahar, but what if he died here, chasing a full-moon fable and she was somewhere else, scared and alone? What if every step he took was one step further away from her?

The hills loomed larger, speckled with what looked like rocks. No, not rocks. Tree stumps. Not a single tree remained standing on the hills.

Only one thing in all of nature destroyed a forest in that way.

Aasim ran with renewed energy. He reached a hill the height of four grown trees and wove between its stumps until he crested the top. A tangled mass of human buildings sprawled into view.

And at the base of the hill crouched the beast.

Aasim ducked behind a stump and peered cautiously around it. Traveler's description had been right, but the beast was even worse than Aasim had imagined. Multiple straight legs angled away unnaturally from the beast's wide belly. Its hide was the color of bark-stripped trees, and it had no tail or nose. On what he'd assumed was its flank but must have been its face, a row of black, sharp-cornered eyes stared unblinking above a gaping, cavernous mouth with its wide brown tongue protruding to the ground.

Humans bustled beside the beast, their thin colorful skins flapping in the gradually growing wind. Aasim counted six of them, all adding strange human items to growing piles. Human scent mounds, perhaps? To keep the beast from entering the city?

There were animals too—snakes, camels, owls. A pair of lions made the nearby herd of sheep bleat nervously, their collective sound the only one that reached Aasim atop the hill. The lions didn't look interested however, and as a seventh human appeared from behind the beast, Aasim saw why.

Ill: Eddy & Claus Linder, Beaver, from the Quadrupeds series (1890), The Metropolitan Museum of Art, New York

The man was tall with a patch of long gray fur beneath his face, and in his paw was a crooked staff. He pointed it at the lions, then the beast. The humid air grew cold as Aasim watched the lions stroll onto the tongue of the beast and disappear in the abyss of its mouth.

The Double-Snatcher pointed his staff at one of the humans' growing mounds. Two brown shapes emerged from behind it, their flat wide tails unmistakable even at this distance.

Nahar!

Aasim's heart leapt to his throat. Nahar headed for the beast with a younger beaver at her side. Aasim darted toward her, but the hill sloped treacherously under his already weak legs. She stepped onto the tongue. His sides heaved with every breath. He wouldn't reach her in time.

"Nahar!" he cried, his voice still too far to be heard. "Nahar!"

She kept walking up into the waiting mouth of the beast until it swallowed her completely.

Aasim skidded to a stop halfway down the hill. His eyes clamped shut, unable to bear the sight of a world without Nahar.

He had failed her. She and their unborn kits were gone.

He thumped his tail against the earth. He thumped again, harder. He continued thumping until he was railing against the ground as if he could transfer his pain to it. The cold despair within him melted as the heat of his wrath took hold. His eyes snapped open.

He wouldn't go home. There was no home without Nahar. He had to avenge her and his children that would never be. He would chew through the Double-Snatcher's staff and destroy the source of his power; no more families would be torn apart this way. Then he would attack the humans. He would bite and scratch as many as he could until he joined Nahar in death.

Aasim resumed his downward path with the focused calm of purpose. The humans continued building their mounds near the mouth of the beast. He'd have to sneak around its backside and attack the Double-Snatcher and his staff from behind.

The Double-Snatcher pointed his staff at the camels, and they plodded toward their doom. As they climbed the tongue, a human exited the mouth and—

Aasim froze. There was an eighth human, and it was *in* the beast's mouth. More than that, it had come *out* of the beast's mouth. Aasim's heart threatened to burst from his chest. If it had survived, maybe Nahar had too.

Aasim crept forward, studying the strange beast more intently. It lay so still, it didn't even seem to breathe.

He gasped. He'd been too far to see it before, but this close, it was obvious. It was no beast with wood-colored skin. It was a lodge. A massive wooden lodge supported not by legs but thick logs braced against the earth. What he'd assumed were eyes must have been ventilation holes.

Its design was impractical. If anything happened to those few supports, the whole structure would topple. He could exploit that weakness and chew through the logs, but Nahar was still inside. He couldn't risk hurting her.

The last of the animals made their way into the lodge, and the humans began carrying items from their mounds into the lodge as well. The Double-Snatcher laid his staff against a rock and hefted a part of a mound himself. Aasim would still attack the staff first. He couldn't risk being mind-snatched if he wanted to free Nahar.

He slunk forward, staying hidden behind stumps until he made a dash for the backside of the lodge. He crept under the support logs to the far end of the structure and peered around its corner. The Double-Snatcher's staff lay abandoned on the rock. Aasim would only have one shot at this.

Once all the humans had their paws full of mound pieces and were facing toward the entrance of the lodge, he ran to the back of the rock and pulled the staff behind it. The rock wasn't large enough to conceal the full length of the wood, but the staff was no thicker than his paw. It would take less than a minute to weaken it enough to snap. He sank his incisors into the middle of the staff and stripped piece after piece, whittling the wood thinner each time.

A chittering human approached the rock. It must have spotted the staff's exposed end, which jostled as he worked. Aasim bit the middle one last time, then bent back one end of the staff with his paws while his tail held down the other.

The staff splintered with a satisfying crack, and the human squealed as it finally spotted him.

Aasim dodged between the human and the rock and ran for the lodge entrance. Chittering erupted among the other humans as he wove between them, pushing his tired muscles to their limits. On the ramp, he startled one human so much it fell, spilling everything it had carried. The human guarding the lodge's entrance ran to help, and Aasim scurried past it into the darkness.

A menagerie of smells overwhelmed him. Every animal he'd ever known and plenty he'd never fathomed stared at him from behind wood-barred walls, each trapped in their own small chamber. They brayed, roared, and bellowed as he ran past, screaming Nahar's name.

"Aasim!" Nahar's voice trilled with relief.

He bounded towards the far end of the lodge where her tiny paws reached between the wooden branches caging her in and skidded to a stop when he reached her. The young male beaver behind her must've been Berosh.

"Don't worry. You're safe now." He bit through four thin branches with one bite each and reached inside for Nahar.

She didn't move.

"We're supposed to be here, Aasim."

She didn't seem the least bit afraid, which terrified him. He'd destroyed the staff. It should have destroyed the power controlling her.

"That's what the Double-Snatcher made you believe," he said.

"It wasn't the Double-Snatcher." Nahar took his paw in hers, and a peaceful smile washed over her. "It was Kastor and Ramad."

They'd rarely spoken of their children since the attack, and the sound of their names stripped him from the inside out. He had to force the words out of a hollow space deep within. "Kastor and Ramad are dead."

"I know. Their spirits came to me." Her continued smile hurt him even more than speaking their names had. "They told me they were alright but danger was coming for us, and I needed to follow them right away. I wanted to wait for you, but they promised you'd follow. They led me here and told me I could trust the humans. And they were right. The humans didn't hurt us."

A group of humans entered the lodge, and Aasim ducked into Nahar's chamber. He lowered his voice. "You only saw what the Double-Snatcher wanted you to see. That's what

Ill: Currier & Ives, Noah's Ark (1868–78),
The Metropolitan Museum of Art, New York

happens when you're mind-snatched, Nahar. Maybe they haven't hurt you yet, but look around." He gripped one of the remaining branches of the cage wall. "It's a trap."

"It was really them," she said. "I felt so much peace."

"If it was really them, why wouldn't they appear to me, too?"

She cocked her head, looking confused. "They didn't?"

"No."

For the first time, he seemed to have broken through her delusion. She scanned the cage around her, and it looked like she was finally seeing reason. When her eyes met his, they held a calm resolve. "I don't know why they didn't visit you, but I do know you came." She squeezed his paw. "Just like they said."

He pulled his paw free. "I didn't come because they said something. I came because you're in danger. Because after frantically scouring the river for clues, I learned that he"—he pointed to Berosh—"had also disappeared, and I feared the heron had been right."

"My grandmother's spirit came to me," Berosh said. "She told me to follow her right away because my future family needed me more than my current one. She promised my parents would be okay."

"They're not okay!" Aasim said. "They're weeping and searching and worried out of their fur."

He poked his head through the cage opening. The humans were rebuilding their mounds in the center of the lodge. He turned back to Nahar and Berosh. "The humans only have a few more loads to carry before their mounds are fully transferred. We have to go now, while they still have their paws full. It's our best chance of escape."

"I know what I saw." Nahar retreated to the far corner of the chamber and lay down beside Berosh. "I'm not leaving. This is where the kits and I will be safe."

The ground beneath Aasim threatened to tear away like their roof in the storm. He'd come all this way, and she wouldn't let him save her.

"Please, Nahar," he begged. "None of it was real."

"You said the same about the Double-Snatcher."

"That's not the same."

"Why not?"

Human chittering blended into the cacophony of animal sounds. Aasim checked the entrance. All eight humans were inside, and only some carried items. The mounds were fully transferred.

They had to run. Now. His tail thumped on the floor faster and faster. How could he get her to see the truth?

Gentle pressure stilled his tail. Nahar stood beside him. She reached up and smoothed the fur on his cheek. "I would never want you to feel trapped." She looked at the open door, then back at him. "It's okay if you need to go."

He didn't know what the humans had planned, but he knew he'd keep her and the kits safe or die trying. He stared at their one chance of escape, not moving as two humans hauled the long wooden ramp into the lodge. The meager light of the outside world was slowly eclipsed by the closing doors until the lodge was lit solely by the dim bars of gray sneaking in through the ventilation holes above.

Nahar squeezed his paw, her voice hopeful. "You believe me then?"

"No." He turned to her. "But that doesn't mean I won't stay."

She rested her head against him, and he held her close while the humans secured a log across the door. Sharp pings attacked the roof, and every creature in the lodge fell silent as the pings swelled into a thundering roar that flooded the air.

The rain had begun.

Originally published in Irreantum *(2023).*

WO HEMSATH writes short stories, poems, novels, and more, with works for both children and adults. She is the author of *Types, Shadows, and Casseroles: Finding Christ in Your Daily Life*, and writes regularly for LDSLiving.com. She is a two-time finalist for the LDSPMA Praiseworthy Awards, holds a BA in screenwriting, has had four pieces place as finalists in various *Mormon Lit Blitz* contests, and has had her work included in university curriculum. When she's not writing, she enjoys teaching at various writing conferences, doing Zumba, and 3D printing new items for her business Fiction & Filament.

Poetry

The Man Who Came Back from the Lunar Colony

Orson Scott Card

To me Earth was always the bright planet,
The blue gleam in a starward window.
But as my feet dragged slower in the moondust
That we had forced to yield us unexpected life,
I could not stop thinking of Earth.
My legs were curious to climb a hill,
My ears to hear the buzzing of a fly.

And so I was the only one to return.
I wasn't blind when I arrived.
I saw the shabbiness, I saw the stains,
I saw the wistful way you face your days,
As if the darkness took you by surprise,
As if the world were fading as you watched.
Hills were only dirt, and, like you,
Within a week I cursed and killed the flies.

Yet I stayed. And still I stay,
Even though I bathe three times a day
And never quite feel clean.
Perhaps it's because here we live
On a world we didn't make ourselves.
Perhaps it's because here we must feel helpless,
For the weather doesn't always go our way.
The dust blows unwelcome in the wind,
A mild punishment for sin, and God,
Who should have been my neighbor out in heaven,
Dwells here in the clutter of nature's randomness.
The sacrament of glory is decay;
The rumble of the traffic is a hymn;
In the dark and the dust and the wind, I bow, I pray.

Originally published in An Open Book (2004).

ORSON SCOTT CARD is the author of the novels *Ender's Game, Ender's Shadow*, and *Speaker for the Dead*. His most recent series are the young adult Pathfinder series, the fantasy Mithermages series, and the Side Step series. Besides these and other science fiction novels, Card has written contemporary fantasy, biblical novels, the American frontier fantasy series *The Tales of Alvin Maker*, poetry, and many plays and scripts. He currently lives in Greensboro, North Carolina, with his wife, Kristine Allen Card.

Essay

A Latter-day Saint Reading of C. S. Lewis's *Perelandra*

CAMERON PRICE

I CAME ACROSS CS LEWIS'S BOOK *Perelandra* about two years ago, while serving as a missionary in Argentina, and was struck by some of the ideas that Lewis explored in it. Here was an author who, while apparently unfamiliar with The Church of Jesus Christ of Latter-day Saints (though he's popular among its members and quoted by its leaders today), portrayed in this book something very similar to the Church's understanding of the Fall of Adam and Eve. I think that his case for his own, more traditional beliefs about the Fall is worthy of serious engagement by Latter-day Saints, even though it was made in an imaginative form, as we try to understand the picture of the Fall given in Restoration scripture and in our temples.

Lewis's *Space Trilogy* is unique in the world of science fiction. Consisting of *Out of the Silent Planet* (1938), *Perelandra* (1943), and *That Hideous Strength* (1945), it follows the protagonist Elwin Ransom as he encounters righteous aliens and wicked men on Mars, prevents the corruption of a paradisiacal Venus, and continues fighting against the forces of evil on Earth. The worldview in this trilogy is explicitly Christian, relatively pessimistic regarding human nature, and even in some ways medieval. Its emphasis on human fallibility and divine glory contrasts sharply with depictions in many works of science fiction of humans as heroes in an indifferent or hostile universe. The books are certainly "soft science fiction" with scientific accuracy deemphasized and supernatural elements introduced. In fact, while reimagining the story of Adam and Eve in *Perelandra*, Lewis deliberately sidestepped questions about the historicity of Genesis and the means of creation, describing Ransom as having "a sensation not of following an adventure but of enacting a myth."* Later, Ransom speculates that the novel's characters representing Adam and Eve may have descended "on the physical [as opposed to the spiritual] side" from <u>sea creatures</u> and wonders about the nature of "the man-like things before men in our own world."† But these were not the most important questions for Lewis, who saw myths as a source of deeper truth than historical facts. This doesn't mean that he always disbelieved in the literal truth of supposed myths. He accepted that inspired scripture could contain genres other than history, but he also accepted the miracles in the Gospels as historical and saw the incarnation of divinity as Jesus as being the incarnation of myth as historical fact. Lewis insisted that the "quality of the real universe" is more like the "divine, magical, terrifying and ecstatic reality" of George MacDonald's works of fantasy rather than the mechanical cosmos that

* CS Lewis, *Perelandra* (Samizdat, 2015), ch. 4, p. 35 (hereafter cited as 4.35).
† Lewis, *Perelandra*, 8.82; Lewis also speculated about the nature of unfallen humans and their predecessors in *The Problem of Pain* (1940).

Ill: James Lewicki, "Perelanda," Copyright Estate of James Lewicki

many infer from modern scientific discoveries.* Lewis's treatment of the creation and Fall narratives should be evaluated on the philosophical and theological ideas that it conveys; speculating about how any of it really worked on a physical level is beside the purpose of the *Space Trilogy*. For this reason, I'll focus on a subject that should interest Latter-day Saint readers more than Lewis's response to scientific materialism: the way his story in *Perelandra* addresses questions related to our own unique theology.

Perelandra begins with Ransom, already an experienced interplanetary traveler, being transported in the nude to the planet Venus (called "Perelandra" in the book's fictional version of the Adamic language) by the "Oyarsa" or governing spirit of Mars. He knows only that he is to serve some purpose there in the struggle between good and evil. For a while he explores the planet alone without meeting any other characters. It's a glorious and colorful paradise whose golden sky is compared to the background of a medieval picture, traditionally representing heavenly light. The land consists of flexible islands floating like mats over the waves of a great ocean.

The first allusion to Genesis comes when Ransom encounters trees with delicious fruit. "Of every tree of the garden thou mayest freely eat."† Throughout the book, fruit is used as a symbol of the good things provided by God and enjoyed by humans. One of the fruits comes in two varieties: a bland, banana-like kind of berry and a kind that looks the same externally but is extremely delicious. Ransom feels inspired to refrain from seeking out the better-tasting ones and eating only that kind, lest the pleasure of eating them be spoiled. Latter-day Saint readers may be reminded here of the similar metaphor in D&C 29:39 and Moses 6:55 about "tasting the bitter" in order to "know the sweet." Both of these use the sense of taste to represent the way that positive experiences can be enhanced by contrast. But the meanings of Lewis's plain fruit and of the Restoration scriptures' bitter taste are subtly different. The verses in D&C and Moses are often associated with the doctrine of "opposition in all things" from 2 Nephi 2 and interpreted to mean that goodness is intrinsically dependent on evil, and specifically that to fully enjoy positive experiences one must know evil and have negative experiences. Lewis, however, considered joy to depend not on sorrow but on restraint and obedience. By

---

* CS Lewis, *George MacDonald: An Anthology* (The Centenary Press, 1946), 21.

† Genesis 2:16.

eating the bland and the delicious berries in their natural proportion, and by showing similar restraint in eating other fruits, Ransom showed gratitude and humility towards the God that provided the fruit and was fit to fully appreciate it. In Lewis's view, people's inability to "know the sweet" without "tasting the bitter" is a consequence of our ungrateful, fallen nature; if we had not fallen we would not need bitterness as the healthy do not need medicine.‡

Having thus already learned theological lessons from the planet itself and its vegetable life, Ransom encounters for the first time a humanoid inhabitant: a green-skinned, nude woman referred to as the Green Lady who it becomes apparent is Perelandra's equivalent of unfallen Eve. Lewis intended this character to be "in some ways like a Pagan goddess and in other ways like the Blessed Virgin," as he described in a letter while writing *Perelandra*.§ This strange description meant that the Lady was to "combine characteristics which the Fall has put poles apart":¶ carefree and unabashed enjoyment of the created world and its pleasures on the one hand, and humility, chastity, and total devotion to God on the other. In conversation with her (such conversations constituting much of the book's plot advancement), Ransom is surprised by her unique way of thinking that defies worldly categories. The saintly Green Lady combines childlike innocence and even ignorance with a wisdom that penetrates to a true understanding of the meaning of things. She does not understand the concept of moral evil or of anything occurring contrary to the will of God (who is called "Maleldil"). But she's aware that her knowledge is limited and is grateful to learn, both through what Latter-day Saints call personal revelation and through her conversations with Ransom. Eventually another character arrives via spaceship on the scene: Weston, the villain of *Out of the Silent Planet*, who serves in Perelandra as a spokesman for the devil and represents the serpent who tempts Eve. He tries to persuade her to live on the only one of Perelandra's islands that is fixed in place rather than floating over the ocean, which she had been

---

‡ Mark 2:17.

§ *Letters of CS Lewis* (Harcourt Brace, 1993), 361.

¶ Ibid.

forbidden by Maleldil to do. This apparently arbitrary commandment represents the biblical prohibition on eating the fruit of the tree of knowledge of good and evil.

The conversation between Weston and the Lady begins with him encouraging her to consider breaking the commandment as a way of gaining wisdom. He presents disobeying the commandment as a brave choice which God really wants her to make:

> "I came here, that you may have Death in abundance. But you must be very courageous."
>
> "Courageous. What is that?"
>
> "It is what makes you to swim on a day when the waves are so great and swift that something inside you bids you to stay on land. . . . But to find Death, and with Death the real oldness [wisdom and experience] and the strong beauty and the uttermost branching out, you must plunge into things greater than waves. . . . Have you understood that to wait for Maleldil's voice when Maleldil wishes you to walk on your own is a kind of disobedience? . . . The wrong kind of obeying itself can be a disobeying."*

At this point Latter-day Saint readers will be reminded of the Lord's insistence in the Doctrine and Covenants that we are not to be "commanded in all things" but should take initiative to do what is right (D&C 58:26–29). This similarity between the malicious Weston's words and our own scripture may bring to mind the way that the devil quoted scripture while tempting Jesus, appealing to true principles but applying them in deceptive ways. Weston continues:

> "There is no good in [this commandment]. Maleldil Himself is showing you that, this moment, through your own reason. . . . Is not Maleldil showing you as plainly as He can that it was set up as a test—as a great wave you have to go over, that you may become really old, really separate from Him[?]"†

Intriguingly, the point of view that Lewis puts into the mouth of Weston is very much like the Latter-day Saint understanding of the Fall. We consider mortal life to be a test, whose purpose includes exercising our moral agency, and we honor Eve for making a courageous choice that fulfilled God's plan rather than foiling it. The disagreement here hinges on the nature of the commandment that Adam and Eve transgressed. Was it in place because Adam and Eve needed to obey it (perhaps to exercise their love and trust of God, which is given near the end of *Perelandra* as the reason for the commandment not to live on the Fixed Land), or was its transgression

---

* Lewis, *Perelandra*, 9.92–93.
† Lewis, *Perelandra* 9.95.

a necessary part of the divine plan? Latter-day Saints hold that the Fall was required for Adam and Eve to have children and bring the human race into the world, as explained in latter-day scripture‡ and in the temple. But why was this the case? Whether or not it involved literally eating a piece of fruit, the Church doesn't teach that the transgression consisted of a sexual act. We don't even describe our fallen state in quasi-biological terms as inherited sin,§ as many Western Christians since St. Augustine have done. It is therefore unclear how exactly the Fall, as 2 Nephi 2 and Moses 5 teach, opened the possibility of our first parents having children. The conflict that Latter-day Saints see between the commandment to "be fruitful and multiply" (Genesis 1:28) and the commandment to not eat from the tree of the knowledge of good and evil (Genesis 2:17) is not addressed in Perelandra, as Lewis included several references to the Green Lady's future children throughout the book, assuming that she could have children without transgressing the equivalent of the latter commandment. However, the book does imply that there's some connection between our fallenness and the state of our sexual nature.

Ransom notes that although he and the beautiful Green Lady are both nude (and both are certainly heterosexual), "embarrassment and desire were both a thousand miles away from his experience."¶ Here as with the pleasures represented by the fruits earlier in the book, the unfallen world is presented as making it easier to avoid overindulgent or transgressive behavior.

That Adam and Eve had to fall in order to have children may be taken as an example of a good thing intrinsically depending on evil things, like in the interpretation of the scriptures on "tasting the bitter" that I mentioned. Lewis would have objected strongly to such an interpretation as he considered evil to be dependent on goodness but not vice versa. In his traditional Christian worldview, the relationship between good and evil is like that of a host and parasite rather than the interdependence of yin and yang; God is not the devil's debtor but his creditor. The portrayal of the Green Lady throughout *Perelandra* is an attempt to show (that is, to imaginatively *show* rather than *tell* like the logical arguments throughout the book do) how this can be true of the good in a person's character and the evil in their experiences. Lewis implies

---

‡ 2 Nephi 2:22–25; Moses 5:10–11.
§ See the second Article of Faith.
¶ Lewis, *Perelandra*, 5.45.

that our spiritual progression could have been accomplished painlessly if the Fall had not occurred. For example, he describes the Lady thus: "[Ransom] knew now what the old painters were trying to represent when they invented the halo. Gaiety and gravity together, a splendour as of martyrdom yet with no pain in it at all, seemed to pour from her countenance."* The implication is that she has the same virtues that in our fallen world are mainly found among people in tribulations and persecutions. Similarly, despite the fact that the Lady has no concept of others' suffering, she "wishe[s] [Ransom], and all things, infinitely well."† Lewis also used the book's dialogue to argue that another specific good, that of having knowledge, does not have to depend on experiencing or doing evil: When Weston insists that the Green Lady must break the commandment in order to learn, Ransom counters that it would be better for her to wait for God to teach her in his own time and his own way.

This point is made again more poetically at the end of the book when the King (a character representing Adam) tells Ransom,

> We have learned of evil, though not as the Evil One wished us to learn. We have learned better than that, and know it more, for it is waking that understands sleep and not sleep that understands waking. There is an ignorance of evil that comes from being young: there is a darker ignorance that comes from doing it, as men by sleeping lose the knowledge of sleep.‡

He says that he "learned of evil and good, of anguish and joy" through revelation and by learning about the Lady's temptations from a distance, without any direct involvement.§ For evil to be in all these ways unnecessary follows logically from the traditional Christian belief that God created the universe out of nothing so that he existed before anything outside himself, meaning that his goodness cannot intrinsically depend on evil as he existed and was perfectly good before there was any evil. But one doesn't need to fully accept traditional Christian metaphysics (Latter-day Saints don't) to object on an emotional level to the idea that goodness fundamentally involves evil. Can't perfect goodness be self-consistent, self-sufficient, and untainted? Can't it be simply bad that things like war and abuse and childhood cancer exist in the world? Hence Lewis's zeal in *Perelandra* to make a case that evil *should not have* ever existed in the cosmos.

---

* Lewis, *Perelandra*, 5.53.
† Lewis, *Perelandra*, 9.92.
‡ Lewis, *Perelandra*, 17.176.
§ Lewis, *Perelandra*, 17.177.

Latter-day Saints can simply reject this view of Lewis's if they wish. After all, he isn't the General Authority that he's treated like! But I find him and similar Christian thinkers persuasive on this point, so I'd like to suggest an alternative way of thinking of the necessity of the Fall within the context of latter-day

This idea fits well with the way that Christ's Atonement is sometimes described as a ransom paid to the forces of evil, which somehow have a claim on Him and His creation. I doubt that this or any other single, systematic explanation can fully explain the mystery of the Atonement, but I think that the ransom theory

> ## Latter-day Saints can simply reject this view of Lewis's if they wish. After all, he isn't the General Authority that he's treated like!

revelation: The presence in the universe of evil, and the unknown reason that our first parents would not have had children or had various other blessings without undergoing some kind of Fall, can be thought of as external constraints within which even God must work. Latter-day Saints sometimes speak of God as working within eternal laws; these may extend beyond the laws that are part of His perfectly good nature, and those that He institutes for His creations, to include such things.¶

has value as an analogy, along with most such theories other than penal substitution. This picture of the Atonement is suggested by the death of Aslan in Lewis's *The Lion, the Witch, and the Wardrobe*, and it's also invoked in *Perelandra* in a way that I'll describe later.

But whatever the ultimate reason is for the Fall being necessary, I'm sure that if it was necessary then it was worth it. It's better to know both joy and suffering than to never live at all, whether the suffering is

---

¶ This way of responding to the problem of evil by putting evil things outside the sphere of God's omnipotence is similar to the description by William James of such things as "elements in the universe which may make no rational whole in conjunction with the other elements, and which . . . can only be considered so much irrelevance and accident—so much 'dirt'" instead of evil being "as Hegel said, . . . an element dialectically required, . . . [to] have a function awarded to it in the final system of truth." *The Varieties of Religious Experience* (Modern Library, 2002), 148–150.

seen as meaningful or senseless. I think it's a strength of the Latter-day Saint understanding of the Fall that it emphasizes this judgement of value so well. Once during my mission, my companion and I were discussing the Plan of Salvation with a person on the street and we mentioned our belief that if Adam and Eve had not fallen, they would not have had posterity. Our interlocutor interpreted this to mean that creating the rest of the human race was "Plan B" for God. We hurried to clarify that God wanted to bring us all into the world and that "all things have been done in the wisdom of him who knoweth all things" (2 Nephi 2:24). The Lord in his wisdom knows that our opportunities to have faith without proof, hope in spite of sorrow, and charity expressed through sacrifice are more valuable than the ease, comfort, and pleasure that we often lack during mortal life.

And there's a passage in *Perelandra* that's quite relevant to this, when Ransom stumbles upon a frog-like creature that had been mutilated by the cruel Weston, the first instance of suffering in that previously spotless world.

> On earth it would have been merely a nasty sight, but up to this moment Ransom had as yet seen nothing dead or spoiled in Perelandra. . . . The milk-warm wind blowing over the golden sea, the blues and silvers and greens of the floating garden, the sky itself—all these had become, in one instant, merely the illuminated margin of a book whose text was the struggling little horror at his feet. . . . It would have been better, or so he thought at that moment, for the whole universe never to have existed than for this one thing to have happened.*

For me, that last sentence rings false, supporting my judgement that the Fall and its consequences must have been worth it. Now, I don't think that what Ransom "thought *at that moment*" is intended to represent his final judgement of the situation, nor Lewis's. Lewis knew that God was right to create the universe and to at least accept the risk of the Fall occurring. When Weston acknowledges that the consequences of the Fall on Earth included valuable opportunities for goodness and heroism, saying that "hardness came of it but also splendour," it's another example of the devil telling (part of) the truth when it serves his purpose.

Just as Latter-day Saints can take into account Lewis's insights, if we so choose, when interpreting our own doctrine of the Fall, I think that a person who fully agrees with Lewis's view of the Fall could profitably accept a certain interpretation of "opposition in all things." This is because even if pain and death and moral evil are

---

* Lewis, *Perelandra*, 9.87–88.

not *absolutely* necessary, it's clear that in our fallen world at least the first two are often *contingently* necessary for our moral development. Since our fallen psychology is not like that of Lewis's Green Lady, we might not develop compassion without seeing the suffering of others, nor the ability to forgive without having been wronged by others. We could not exercise courage without danger nor patience without frustration, and as I've described, we often can't appreciate our blessings without "tasting the bitter." The virtues that we do have must usually be put to the test by real, stretching experience to become strong and enduring. To quote a verse from George MacDonald:

> Remember, Lord, thou hast not made me good.
> Or if thou didst, it was so long ago
> I have forgotten—and never understood,
> I humbly think. At best it was a crude,
> A rough-hewn goodness, that did need this woe,
> This sin, these harms of all kinds fierce and rude.
> To shape it out, making it live and grow.†

So whatever counterfactual statements one makes about what would've happened without the Fall, whether those of Lewis or those of Lehi,‡ the current state of the world is governed by the principle of "opposition in all things." In fact, a lot of the greatest goodness is occasioned by the greatest evil—the ultimate example of this being the death of Christ that became the means of our redemption.

Towards the end of the book, Ransom determines that it's his terrible duty to save the Lady from further temptation and prevent Perelandra's Fall by having a fight to the death with Weston. He finds it hard to believe that God would allow the fate of that world to depend on his own actions, but he perceives the voice of God in his mind refuting each of his rationalizations and making it impossible for him to deny that it does, for the worlds were created in such a way that important things in them were to hinge on human choice. Raising the stakes even more, the Voice says to him, "My name also is Ransom."§ He realizes that this means not only that Christ had been the ransom for sin on Earth but also that He would do it again in Perelandra if Ransom chose not to perform his duty. Ransom "reali[zes] the true width of the frightful freedom that was being put into his hands" and then resolves to do it.¶ And thus in this chapter, which is more profound

---

† George McDonald, *Diary of an Old Soul* (Project Gutenberg, 2013), daily verse for October 1. Compare Genesis 1:31.
‡ 2 Nephi 2:22-23.
§ Lewis, *Perelandra*, 11.122.
¶ Ibid.

than I can do justice to here, Lewis affirmed a principle that is central to the Latter-day Saint faith: the crucial importance of our agency, which God will respect however it challenges us and whatever it costs Him.

After considering agency and the Fall in great depth for most of the book, Lewis widens his focus in the last chapter—another remarkable one—to touch on the cosmic scope of the Plan of Salvation. While conversing with the Green Lady, the King, and the Oyarsa of Perelandra, Ransom expresses dismay about the overwhelming scale of what can look like a meaningless universe. What divine purpose can there be in a cosmos consisting mostly of empty space and uninhabited planets? And how can our own little corner of the universe and the relatively short lifespan of the human race be at the center of it all? I've had similar questions myself: isn't it mathematically a zero-probability event for the present finite stretch of time to be special out of all eternity, or for our own world to be special out of an infinite creation?* Ransom's interlocutors respond that the unique significance of a particular part of creation is a function of one's perspective. Each part of creation may from its own point of view be regarded as the center, including humans and the other creatures and even the inanimate matter. The inhabitants of Earth see the incarnation of Christ on this planet as the central event of cosmic history, but for newer worlds like Perelandra all the events of Earth's history are merely a prequel to their own. If the divine plan, as Boyd K. Packer said, is like a three-act play, its various characters may regard different scenes as the central ones. And what we think of as its denouement is merely the beginning of the real play—the unending (and perhaps timeless) heavenly story that Lewis dubs the "Great Dance."

Lewis's description of this is in the spirit of "If You Could Hie to Kolob."† And this passage has a few curious details that parallel latter-day teachings. There's a reference to "Maleldil and . . . His Father,"‡ implying that the name for God that had been used throughout the book refers specifically to God the Son—which is what Latter-day Saints believe about Jehovah in the Old Testament. It's acknowledged that at any time the Lord has multiple

---

* See Moses 7:36.
† See also Sydney Carter's hymn "Lord of the Dance" and the traditional English carol "Tomorrow Shall Be My Dancing Day."
‡ Lewis, *Perelandra*, 17.177, 179.

worlds that are in different stages of their history.§ And yet divine glory is qualitative rather than quantitative, in an interesting contrast to rhetoric about "eternal increase" of kingdoms and posterity: "They who add years to years in lumpish aggregation, or miles to miles and galaxies to galaxies, shall not come near His greatness."¶ Earlier in the book the Green Lady says that all the intelligent inhabitants of the worlds that would be created in the future would be humanoid because God had become Man, which is not far from our own teaching that "the inhabitants [of the worlds] are begotten sons and daughters unto God" (D&C 76:24) and therefore are made in His image even on a physical level.

And while Latter-day Saints sometimes disparage certain traditional Christian metaphorical pictures of heaven (similar to that in Mosiah 2:28 and Mormon 7:7) as flat and uninteresting compared to our own robust understanding of the afterlife, Lewis makes it clear that he understands the nature of the next life to be something vibrant and active, if beyond our mortal capacity to fully comprehend. While sometimes disagreeing with aspects of the theology of the Restoration, CS Lewis used his keen mind and imaginative faculty to declare truths with which Latter-day Saints agree: that the way that we use our agency is of crucial importance and that the Lord's works surpass our wildest imaginations "as the heavens are higher than the earth." Likewise, while we are certain to sometimes disagree with him, his writings are an excellent source of ideas to ponder while pursuing further light and knowledge.

------

§ See Moses 1:35-38; Lewis also speculated about the possibility of God creating and redeeming many worlds in *Miracles* (1947, revised 1960).
¶ Lewis, *Perelandra*, 17.181.

CAMERON PRICE was born in Salt Lake City but grew up in Allentown, Pennsylvania and served in the Argentina Buenos Aires South Mission where he preferred his yerba mate without sugar. He is a sophomore studying chemistry at BYU, but his insatiable curiosity is not confined to one subject. When not studying, reading, or otherwise overthinking things, he likes to play outside and enjoy the majesty of the outdoors. He loves his family and friends.

Poetry

THE FALLEN

DA COOPER

Not even the devils are evil by nature
—St. Thomas Aquinas

I see them from my perch
atop the ever-burning church

that stands next to the square
in uptown Dis. They aren't aware,

it seems, that they are being
watched. Malicious eyes farseeing

through ashen mist and gloom
peak out of every smoldering tomb

they pass. I watch them meet
a tortured shade down on the street,

stopping their hurried walk
to introduce themselves and talk.

Although I am not near
enough to hear their voices, cheer

erupts out of their faces,
irrupting in the hellish places

they pass—the residue
it leaves is something I once knew.

I dig around my mind—
they're wandering preachers, nuns, some kind

of monks. No, missionaries!
And as they rove about, each carries

a bag of pamphlets, books
they give to anyone who looks

them in the eyes too long.
They always say that they "belong

to the Church of..." what?
I can't recall the name. I shut

*Ill: Gustave Doré, detail from illustration to Dante's Inferno,
Canto XXIII: "Scarcely had his feet" (1857)*

my eyes to concentrate.
What is that word they say they hate,

but really love? It's Moron,
right? No, that's not it. Or mon-

ist, maybe? No. What is
that word? The Devil says that his

epiphanies all come
when he stops straining, so I hum

a little tune and try
to dream of other things. But why

is it so hard to think
with them nearby? A twisted kink

is tangling up my thoughts
into a mass of Gordian knots.

Maybe I've been below
too long? Come on, I know

this word... I've got it! Mormon!
Now they approach the demon doorman

who guards the graveyard gates
and ask to enter. But he hates

everyone, so I know
that he'll say no, tell them to go

to heaven. But... he smiles
instead. He smiles? I've watched the miles

of shades go filing in,
each to be punished for some sin.

How many have I seen
plead with that fiend, and some obscene

remark or gesture was
his only reply because

his hatred is so strong
for them? My God, it's been so long

since I have heard real laughter—
not since I entered the hereafter

and took the broad path down
into this ugly, stinking town.

There they go, door to door,
searching out the needy, poor

of spirit—those whose will,
though bad, is malleable still—

whose hearts are sad and broken,
open enough to show some token

of sorrow, of remorse
for their soul-piercing sins. Of course,

I don't care about
their creed—I've never had a doubt,

I've always been content
to sit up on this monument

to faith and hope gone wrong
and watch the torment of the throng

of sinners down below—
the endless, fetid ebb and flow

of suffering and pain,
siphoning spirits down the drain.

But something's different now,
changed. I don't know why or how.

I touch my face and feel
a tear, then bend myself to kneel

upon the roof, my eyes
searching for heaven through the skies

kept dark by pitch-black clouds.
I jump down, swoop over the crowds

of shades, landing as close
as possible to them. That gross

charred-flesh smell emanates
out of the fiery tombs. The fates

arranged a funny joke
this time—to make me want to poke

Ill: Gustave Doré, illustration to Dante's Inferno, Canto III:
"Abandon all hope ye who enter here" (1857)

my nose in missionary
business. I land beside them very

softly so neither notes
my coming. Then, I grab their throats.

What are you doing here
in Dis? I howl, try to appear

as menacing, as scary
as I can. "I'm a missionary,"

one gags, with curious
good cheer. I roar in furious,

pretended agitation.
This is the city of damnation

for shades deprived of light,
destined to dwell in darkest night

forever, so I ask
again, why are you here, what task

were you sent here to do
among the hopeless damned? The two

of them grab at my fingers.
A small part of my anger lingers

as I release my grasp
from off their little necks. They gasp

for breath, upon their knees,
then stand as one, and, with a wheeze,

one says, "We represent
Jesus Christ. We have been sent

to call all to repent,
to preach unto the malcontent

deliverance from sin."
I feel a tingling on my skin.

There is no liberation,
no rescue from the desperation

of Hell. No one gets out
of here. There is no hope, I shout

with rage. Didn't you see
the sign when you came in? A sea

of frenzied feelings splashes
over my heart. Hellfire's ashes

fall like snow and stay
fixed on their faces. Go away.

There's nothing in this place
for you. They stand unmoved. "The grace

of God is all you need.
God makes the weak things strong. A seed

starts small, but it will grow.
Just plant it in your heart. I know

that Christ can change us all."
I smirk. I know the words of Paul

and Alma too, but they
do not apply down here. The day-

light cannot penetrate
the darkness nor its mists of hate

which permeate our air.
They nod, but do not seem to care

what I say. "God's plan
gives every single fallen man

and woman the chance to change."
A passing pang of sadness, strange

though poignant, darts across
my face. And so, I quickly toss

my head the other way.
I'm not sure if they saw. They say

again, "Anyone can
repent, any woman or man

who ever lived." I've caught
them in a puzzle now. I'm not

alive, and I have never
been born. I smile at my clever

retort. Frustratingly,
their smiles do not droop. You see,

I was cast down to Hell
after the War, and here I dwell

as punishment forever.
We fallen angels will not ever

be drawn out of this pit.
"Sister," says one, "I must admit

I think the demon's right.
Unfortunately, Jesus' light

can't reach the hosts who followed
Satan in Heaven. They were swallowed

by death and can't be saved.
I was told they're too depraved."

A sadness grips my heart.
You see, I say, now go. Depart!

The other one replies
with boldness, staring in my eyes:

"No. That can't be true.
This angel is God's child, like you

and me." She thinks a moment,
"Is it an infinite atonement

or isn't it?" We sit
in brooding silence. "It

is written that God cures
all wounds. I think that can mean yours

too if you want it to.
I know Christ can change even you,

can heal your soul and feed it."
I turn away. Shut up and beat it!

I yell and try to mope,
but she will not abandon hope.

"This is why we were sent
by our mission president,

to preach to all the fallen.
This is our calling and we're all in,

right, sister?" Now the other,
mind changed, chimed in: "Right. You're our brother,

a child of God with worth
beyond your understanding. Birth

upon the earth and life
in Christ await. Give up this strife

you chose so long ago.
Forgiveness will be yours. I know,

we know, that everything
is possible with God." The spring

of hope begins to thaw
my icy heart. What of the law?

"We know and testify
you can be healed." Now they both cry.

"All things are possible
in Christ, no gulf's uncrossable

for him." I'll think about
your words, I say. They then pull out

a book, hand it to me.
"If you read this book you'll be

forever changed." I look
at it. You know, I've read this book

before. "Read it this time
with your mind open to the rhyme

of spirit meeting spirit.
God's voice is in it. You will hear it

calling out to you.
Be open to it being true."

I'll try, I say, sincerely.
"And don't forget, God loves you dearly,"

one says. And then the other
smiles again and calls me 'brother.'

"We'd also love to see you
come to church. I guarantee you

that you will feel God's love."
Where is this church? "It's up above

in Limbo. If you want,
we'll walk with you, it can be daunt—"

I know the way, I say
a bit too quickly. Anyway,

I'll fly. And I unfold
my wings. She smiles. "Of course." I hold

the book a little tighter.
"Our branch president's a writer.

I think you'll get along."
Doubtful. We demons don't belong

up there. The shades get nervous.
"Not him. He likes to be of service,

and sometimes he will guide
folks out past Satan's underside.

He's hiked down all the levels,
and so he's met a lot of devils."

I smile, then laugh out loud.
I know that's definitely not allowed.

I'll have to meet this guy.
I swear to come, then say goodbye.

My heart is pricked with hope,
as I watch them climb the slope.

I look up through hell's haze—
it clears, and starlight fills my gaze.

Ill: Gustave Doré, illustration to Dante's Inferno,
Canto II: "Day was departing" (1857)

DA COOPER is a poet from Houston, Texas. His LDS-themed poetry (speculative and otherwise) has appeared in *ARCH-HIVE*, *Dialogue*, *Irreantum*, *Ships of Hagoth*, and *Wayfare*. He is happy to have recently joined the *Further Light* team as the poetry editor.

Fiction

Charity Never Faileth

Jaleta Clegg

Sister Thomas, thank you so much." Pam Jensen accepted the glass pan full of gently quivering green gelatin. Carrot shreds mocked her from the glistening depths.

Sister Thomas waved her hand. "I'd love to stay and help, Pam, but Jared and Omner have basketball practice and little Tiffany has her piano lessons and Sariah wants to be picked up at the high school in half an hour. You know how life is. Toodles!" Her designer sweats disappeared rapidly through the glass door of the church kitchen.

Pam sighed. Another lime gelatin salad. How many was that now? Twenty three? She set the pan on the counter next to the fridge. She wasn't sure how many would actually fit in the fridge. She'd have to do some juggling.

"Sister Jensen? I hate to bother you, but . . ."

Pam stopped her eyes from rolling with a supreme effort of will at the sound of the breathy voice. She'd recognize it anywhere. But, charity suffereth long, and all that. She pasted a smile on her face as she turned around. "Yes, Sister Love?"

Nyra Love waddled to the cabinets, one hand spread across her extremely pregnant belly. "I just need a pitcher of water, you know, for the little ones, when they come." She smiled her vapid smile, like a brain-damaged hamster. Her soft voice grated on

Pam's already stretched nerves. "I hope you don't mind."

"No, no problem, Nyra. Are you sure you should be helping tonight? Wasn't your baby due Sunday?"

Nyra Love giggled. "Oh, no. I was due last Thursday but the doctor says all first babies are late. It's my responsibility to be here, it's my calling, to serve in the nursery at Relief Society weekly enrichment meetings." A frown crawled over her face. "What are we supposed to call them now?"

"Just call it a birthday dinner. Do you want help?" Pam wedged Sister Thomas's gelatin offering into the fridge with the other green masses. All had carrots. A few sported pineapple tidbits or canned pears. Sour cream covered two with a thick layer of 'frosting'.

Nyra pressed her hand to her belly. "Oh, that was a strong one. Nothing to worry about, Sister Jensen. It's only Braxton-Hicks." She waddled from the room, a plastic pitcher clutched in her free hand.

Pam shook her head as she began arranging fresh fruit. Rainbows sounded fun, especially for March. Blueberries, kiwi, pineapple, mandarin oranges because they were easier than orange slices, with a border of strawberries. But that left out violet. What fruit could she add this late, though? It would mean yet another trip to the store. She eyed the carefully carved pineapple boats sitting empty next to the trays. Maybe she should just mix it all and fill up the boats. A faint gurgle across the kitchen caught her attention. She paused, glancing over the simmering crockpots of ham. "Must have been the lids rattling." She popped open a container of strawberries. If she mixed it all up, the sisters would never notice purple missing and if they did, well, that was their problem. Boats with mixed fruit it would be. And maybe one tray with a rainbow, for fun.

Edith Merkel stumped through the door, her orthotically correct shoes squeaking on the linoleum floor. "You want real forks or them plastic atrocities?"

"Just use the real ones, please."

Edith yanked the drawer open, extracting fistfuls of flatware. "Where's your committee at? Lazing around expecting those of us humble enough to serve to wait on them hand and foot." Forks protruded from her fingers.

"I'm sure they had important things to do." Pam arranged a ring of strawberries on the tray. The committee members had all made excuses when they saw Edith's name on the list. Sister Merkel's tongue was legend in the Fifth Ward.

"More important than helping us set up this dinner they expect to eat?" The elderly woman stumped from the kitchen, muttering under her breath.

Pam spooned mixed fruit into the pineapple shells. She debated calling Sister Harris for help. No, Sister Harris made Nyra look intelligent by comparison. Another rattle sounded from the general direction of the refrigerator. Pam jumped, startled by the unexpected noise. She glanced nervously around the room. Everything looked all right. She turned the crockpots to low, then gathered the fruit rainbow and the pineapple boats, carrying them to the gym.

Sister Merkel's ironing board, complete with ancient avocado green iron, sat front and center by the food tables. The iron puffed out steam, like an asthmatic wheezing. Pam made a mental note to remove them as soon as possible. Before she tripped on the cord.

Edith was stomping around each table, slamming forks on paper napkins. Her tightly permed white hair gleamed with blue highlights under the fluorescent fixtures. "I ironed each and every one of these cloths and they still have wrinkles. That's what comes of storing them in a cupboard. They don't make them like they used to, no, they certainly don't."

"They look beautiful, Sister Merkel." Pam set her burden on the dessert table.

"Where do you want these?" Edith slapped bunches of silk flowers on the table. "I got most of the tables but there's more left over. Can't even have decent flowers these days. Have to use these fake ones. In my day, we just plucked them from our yards. Everyone grew flowers then, not like these days."

Thumps sounded from the direction of the kitchen. Pam glanced over her shoulder at the door. "It's March, Sister Merkel. The flowers are still buried under six inches of snow."

"Well, I can't be having these fake things dropping what-all into my drink."

Pam nodded at the serving table, still empty of food but with serving utensils marking space. "Just set them there. We can arrange them down the center once we get the food out."

Breathless screams shattered the peace of the church building.

Nyra bolted inside the gym. The pregnant woman yanked on the doors, which resisted. Nyra threw anxious glances at the slowly closing doors as she fluttered across the gym. "It ate the little ones' snacks! Every last box!"

"What did, Nyra?" Pam hurried to her side.

"It was hideous, all big and blobby looking!"

Edith nodded her head, curls bobbing as she said, "I'd bet on the bishop, if I was a betting woman, which I'm not."

"Not the bishop." Nyra's voice wavered. She tugged her blond braid.

"Then what, Nyra?" Did pregnancy produce hallucinations? Pam's never had. She patted the younger woman's arm. Nyra was flighty at the best of times, though, so maybe this was normal for her.

"That!" Nyra pointed at the far door.

Green gelatin oozed between through the double door, assembling into a wobbling mass. Carrot shreds and cheddar fish crackers danced in its middle.

Edith squinted at the blob. "Just like the summer of seventy-one. Back in Tooele, you know. We were setting up for a dinner just like this. Someone decided it would be tasty to put pears and pineapple in the same salad with the carrots. Some things should never be done."

The quivering mass of lime gelatin extended a pseudopod, inching across the wood floor. The sour cream topping rolled together, extruding out the top of the blob. Half a canned pear popped out the middle, like the pupil of an eyeball. The three women inched backwards.

"It's formed an eye!" Edith clutched her flowers. "This is a bad one."

"This happened before?" Pam asked, her attention fixed on the pulsing blob of gelatinous salad.

Edith nodded vigorously. "It's an abomination, like Daniel said would come haunting us for our sinful ways."

They backed to the serving tables, taking refuge behind the desserts. The gelatin oozed slowly across the floor towards them, carrot shreds undulating inside.

Pam cleared her throat. Fear made her voice tremble. "How did you stop it back then, Edith?"

> **"Someone decided it would be tasty to put pears and pineapple in the same salad with the carrots. Some things should never be done."**

"We lured it out to the parking lot. Late July in Tooele. Thing melted."

Nyra pressed both hands to her belly. "My, that was a strong one."

"How far apart are the contractions?" Pam asked.

The blob quivered to a stop in the center of the gym. The eye extended upwards on a dripping stalk of green gelatin. It scanned the room, dripping shreds of carrot.

"About every five minutes for the last two hours," Nyra answered. "The doctor says this baby won't come until next week, though."

Edith thumped her fist on the table. "Sweetheart, you're in labor. I birthed five of my own. Your doctor is an idiot."

Nyra's lip trembled. "But I can't have the baby now. I'm supposed to be teaching the children's class. Ooo." Her eyes widened. Her fists clutched the table for support.

Edith tossed her flowers on the serving table. "Just breathe, honey."

Pam absently patted Nyra's back. The gelatin monster oozed closer, leaving slimy trails of carrot on the floor. A fish cracker plopped from the eyestalk.

"Hahahee?" Nyra panted uncertainly.

"It's too cold to melt that thing," Pam said to Edith.

"We could try wrapping it in a tablecloth and flushing it," Edith suggested.

"Hahahee!" Nyra grabbed Pam's hand, squeezing hard.

Pam winced at the strength of Nyra's grip. She edged the pregnant woman behind the serving tables—two long ones set with a small space between. The dessert one held her fruit rainbow, pineapple boats, and an unfilled chocolate fountain. Edith's ironing board stood proudly front and center. Still so much to do and no time to deal with rebellious gelatin salads. "How are we going to possibly find a tablecloth big enough to wrap that?"

Nyra panted. The joints in Pam's hand popped. Pam pulled her hand free before Nyra damaged it permanently.

"Try singing, honey. It helped me." Edith fingered the extra forks laid out on the serving table.

"Tell me the stories of Jesus, I love to heehee HA!" Nyra squeezed tears from her eyes. "I don't want my baby to be born in a church gym."

Pam patted her pocket. Her cell phone was at home, where she usually left it for church activities. "I'll slip out and call your husband." Two smaller green blobs oozed through the side doors. "Or not."

Five more small blobs oozed into the gym, sliding out in a wide semicircle behind the big one.

"They're flanking us." Edith hunched behind the chocolate fountain. "Did some idiot add marshmallows? No wonder they can think!" She flipped a fork at the largest blob. It hung, vibrating gently, among the pears.

Nyra pulled away from Pam's support. She drew herself to her full five-foot three height, chin set. "As sisters in Zion, we all work to-heeheeHA!" She grabbed a wedge of fresh pineapple, flinging it at the monstrous blob. Her quavering

"Did some idiot add marshmallows? No wonder they can think!"

soprano carried on, pausing only for panting breaths. "The heeheeHA of his blessings we heeheeHA!" Another wedge of pineapple struck the monster.

The green gelatin stopped, wobbling in place. Burbling moans echoed through the room.

"I think you hurt it." Edith winced at a high note.

"You're a genius, Nyra!" Pam reached for the fruit rainbow.

"I am?" Nyra smiled, like a ray of sunshine breaking through a storm. "We have been born as heeheeHA of old." A rain of pineapple struck the blob.

Rivulets of green liquid dripped from the wounds inflicted by the fresh fruit.

Pam grinned at Edith. "Never put fresh or frozen pineapple, kiwi, or papaya in gelatin." She plucked a wedge of pineapple from the carefully arranged tray. "Take that!" Her slice landed on the floor several feet in front of one of the smaller blobs.

"You need a bit more enthusiasm. Or better weaponry." Edith squatted behind the table, digging through her baggy pockets.

The quivering mound of green gelatin retreated a few inches, oozing back until it encountered a table. Green slime sucked the place settings and fake flowers inside the lump.

"That's going to leave a stain!" Edith's eyes hardened.

Pam shifted more fruit into Nyra's reach. The young mother-to-be snatched an empty pineapple shell, lobbing it across the gym.

"I belong to the heeheeheeee HAAAAA!"

The quarter pineapple shell, carefully hollowed with the leaves still attached, struck the blob in its bobbing sour cream eye. The eyestalk retracted, dragging the pineapple inside. The thing pulsed, like a heartbeat. A warbling, burbling croak emerged from the interior.

"You've hurt it now, honey." Edith emerged from behind the table. She clutched a contraption of two forks and several rubber bands in one hand.

"What is that?" Pam nudged more pineapple in Nyra's direction.

Edith wedged a pineapple slice in the dangling rubber bands. "Wrist rocket. I spent twenty-seven years with the Cub Scouts. I can make anything into a weapon." She spun on the ball of her orthotically clad foot, letting the pineapple fly at one of the smaller blobs creeping along the wall. "Take that, foul fiend!"

The smaller blob dissolved into a puddle. Carrot shreds floated listlessly over the wood floor.

"Poor thing." Pam rose on tiptoes to peer at it.

Edith snorted as she reloaded. "That thing would have eaten you. Don't waste pity on that nasty salad."

"Onward Christian heeheeheeeee, marching as to war!" Pineapple rained down on the blob from both of Nyra's hands.

The burbling croak rose in pitch. The six smaller blobs slithered to the main monster. It absorbed them, growing larger and taller with each addition. Streams of unset gelatin dripped from gaping holes left by the pineapple, like blood from wounds.

Nyra sent the last pineapple boat sailing across the gym. The creature howled when it hit. Goo splattered the nearby tables.

Nyra placed both hands on her belly. "We're out of pineapple. What are we going to do?"

"Ninja kiwi attack!" Edith grabbed a handful of kiwi slices. Her shoes squeaked as she darted from behind the table, racing towards the blob.

"Be careful, Sister Merkel!" Pam could barely watch.

"Kill it!" Nyra shrieked.

Edith slowed halfway to the monster. "Dang my artificial knee!" She limped bravely forward, the kiwi clutched to her bosom.

The far door of the gym opened. The bishop, a stout man who dearly loved his food and never missed a Relief Society dinner, peered inside. "Is everything all right, sisters?"

Nyra turned to Pam, her rabbity face creased with concern. "You have to stop it, Sister Jensen, or it's going to eat them both. Oh dear. Hee. Haaaa. Aaaaaaugh!" She bent double over the table, hands pressed to her belly.

"I don't know how! The fruit's gone." Pam dithered, eyes searching for anything that might help. She caught sight of the iron, still plugged in and gently steaming. Edith's iron was a massive old relic from the fifties, the kind that had been discontinued for safety reasons.

Pam yanked the plug from the wall, hefting the beast with both hands.

"Lovely centerpiece thing. What is it?" The bishop wandered closer to the undulating blob of green gelatin.

"Don't touch it! It's evil!" Edith limped closer.

The blob extended a pseudopod, reaching for the old woman's bobbing white head.

"Oh no, you don't, you Canaanite monstrosity!" Edith thrust the handful of kiwi at the reaching tentacle, parrying the monster's attack.

At the same time, the bishop reached one hand to the quivering backside of the monster. The sour cream eye, pineapple still embedded, rolled through the blob towards him.

"Stop, Bishop Alger! Oh, please stop!" Pam closed her eyes, breathed a hasty prayer, then rushed at the blob, iron held before her like a weapon. She hadn't actually run for fifteen years. Her middle-aged body protested even while adrenaline spurred her on.

"Heee heeeeee heeeeee HAAAA-AAAA!" Nyra's scream reached a new pitch.

The blob shivered, ripples cascading over its surface in time to Nyra's panting screeches. Vague recollections of resonant frequencies and shattering wine glasses surfaced in Pam's mind as she raced closer, the heat of the iron scorching her fingers.

The gelatin salad extruded a mass of carrot shavings onto the bishop's hand just as Edith sprayed the other side with kiwi. The thing howled.

Pam plunged the hot iron into the center of the blob as Nyra's scream reached maximum volume. The blob of gelatin exploded. Carrot shavings, cheddar fish, canned pears, and pineapple tidbits rained across the room in a sudden silence.

The bishop blinked, staring at the green destruction splattered across the gym. He brushed his hand absently across the green staining his once-white shirt. "Dinner isn't quite ready yet? Carry on, sisters. I'll be in my office." He blinked again, then wandered from the gym.

Edith scowled at the goop on the floor. "I'll get a mop."

"Sister Jensen?" Nyra stumbled from behind the dessert table. "I think I should go to the hospital now. My doctor was wrong."

Pam hurried to the young woman's side, offering a supportive hand. "I'll call your husband."

Nyra smiled her sweetly innocent smile, only now it had teeth and a backbone. "You tell him

we're naming our little boy Lee. Brother Lee Love."

Pam patted Nyra's hand. "That's a sweet name." Pam's gaze traveled over the scattered decorations, covered with gobbets of melting gelatin. She shook her head, still not quite sure what had happened. But, she thought as she straightened her spine, put your shoulder to the wheel and they would have it all tiptop in no time.

She gently led Nyra from the gym. Dessert would be a bit scanty, but she had a few more strawberries for the chocolate fountain she could use. They had rolls and funeral potatoes to go with the ham. Dinner would be plentiful as always without the blob. No one ever ate the green gelatin salad anyway.

A version of this piece was originally published in Monsters & Mormons (2011) *and reprinted in* Brain Candy (2013).

JALETA CLEGG loves finding the absurd in the everyday, then making up stories about it. She writes space opera, fantasy, silly horror, and whatever else catches her fancy. Find links to her work at www.jaletac.com.

Call for Submissions

Be part of the next issue of Further Light!

Fiction: 1000-8000 words; science fiction, fantasy, and related genres
Nonfiction: 3000-word target; creative nonfiction or literary analysis of speculative fiction with a Latter-day Saint connection
Poetry: up to three poems at a time; speculative and religious elements
Art: send portfolios to editor@furtherlightmag.com

Deadlines
Issue 2: submit by February 28, 2026; responses by March 31, 2026
Issue 3: submit by August 31, 2026; responses by September 31, 2026

Payment & Rights
$25 honorarium to published fiction and nonfiction
$10 honorarium to published poetry
Authors will receive a free copy of each print issue where their work appears

PG-13 rating or below
No AI-generated work of any kind
Reprints OK; Simultaneous Submissions OK

More information at www.furtherlightmag.com/p/submissions
Questions? Email editor@furtherlightmag.com

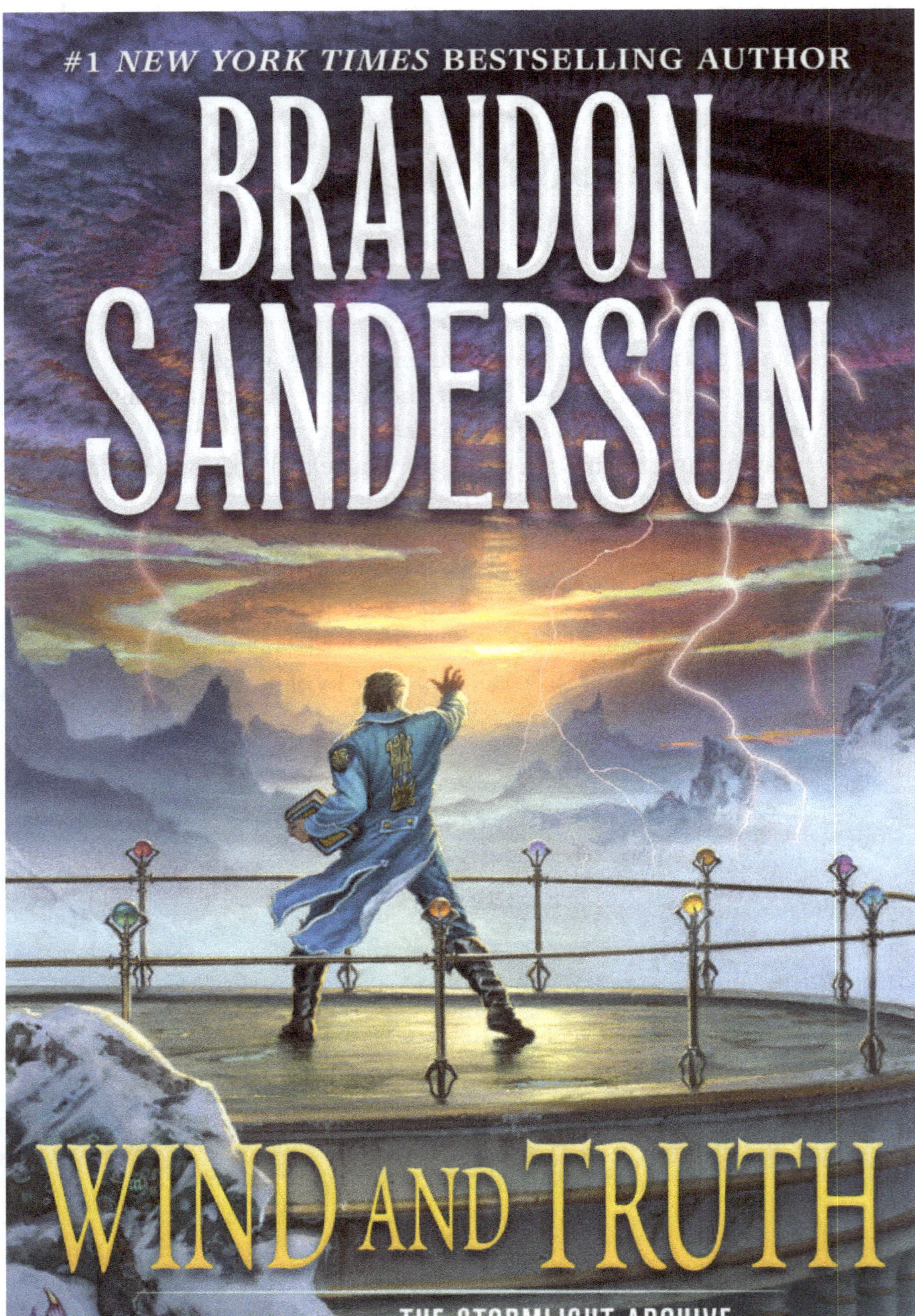
#1 NEW YORK TIMES BESTSELLING AUTHOR
BRANDON SANDERSON
WIND AND TRUTH
BOOK FIVE OF THE STORMLIGHT ARCHIVE

Essay

Journey Before Destination, Faith Before Certainty

Experiencing Belief in Wind and Truth

Liz Busby

This essay contains spoilers for the first arc of the Stormlight Archive.

I DON'T THINK IT WOULD BE incorrect to say that *Wind and Truth* is Brandon Sanderson's most controversial book to date. Part of this is the sheer length of the volume: the more-than-1300 pages stretch the patience of even hardcore fans of epic fantasy. Though previous volumes have also been behemoths, this one also felt it, with a plot that rushed readers from one side of Roshar to the other and yet seemed at the same time to drag on and on. Many readers of *Wind and Truth* noticed a certain repetitiveness to Sanderson's language, leading to the thought that Sanderson's editors ought to have done more cutting. An irritating increase in

modernisms also placed this book out of sync with previous works in the series. Characters who were "courting" in previous books are now said to be "dating" and eventually become "exes." In a society where the majority of people don't have watches or clocks, a character tells another to wait "just a sec."

One particularly awkward example of this trend is the insertion of the modern concept of "therapy" into the book's medieval/early Renaissance-ish setting. While these characters have always been identifiable as suffering from mental illness, the in-world language tended to be archaic—"battle shock," "melancholia." In the previous volume, Kaladin invented the idea of group talk therapy but never referred to it as anything other than being a different kind of "surgeon." In *Wind and Truth*, however, the term "therapist" appears as the punchline of a joke at an otherwise climactic moment. Granted, it's introduced by Hoid, a character who has reason to know more modern terminology, but the contrast has been jarring to many readers. If the goal of fantasy is to be immersive, the sprinkling of modern language in this book breaks that immersion.

Do these imperfections mean *Wind and Truth* is doomed to be remembered as a rushed and forgettable mid-season finale in the Stormlight Archive? During the last year, I've wrestled through the book a second time, and I've come to believe that if we can look beyond some of its rough edges, the fifth volume of the Stormlight Archive may be one of the most profound books in the series. *Wind and Truth* asks many questions that, to me, seem directly attached to deeply Latter-day Saint theology. And it answers these questions in ways that are particularly insightful into how faith operates in the modern world.

For example, one subject that Sanderson grapples with in this series is what an "infinite and eternal sacrifice" (Alma 34:10) actually looks like and why it had to be done by a divine being rather than a mortal human. In the world of Roshar, humanity fights against the continually reincarnating spirits of their enemies bent on vengeance. In order to prevent the planet from being embroiled in eternal war—hard to win a war if your enemies can't die—ten individuals choose to use their souls to construct a spiritual barrier protecting the planet. In *Wind and Truth*, we see these people, who become the semidivine Heralds, willingly agree to endure "endless torment" (D&C 19:6) by these enemy spirits in order to protect their fellows. At first, the Heralds are able to last under this torment for centuries, but the accumulation of physical and mental anguish eventually builds up to the point where their merely human capacity breaks. When they are no longer able to "drink the bitter cup, and shrink" (D&C 19:18), they give up their protection of the planet and the cycle of reincarnation restarts, the devastating conflict resumes.

Wind and Truth spends a lot of its pages focusing on exactly what this requirement of an infinite sacrifice does to a merely human soul. The novel lets us witness the moment of idealism and desperation that led to the forging of this pact. Yet as characters interact with the Heralds as they exist in the present day, it is apparent that they are broken people, warped by their attempt to sacrifice beyond what was endurable. Where each Herald was seen as representing a classical virtue, they now display the opposite vice: Kalak's judgement gives way to indecision, Shallash's artistic creation to destruction, Ishar's leadership to tyranny, Batar's wise counsel to corrupt flattery. As a reader, when I see how this attempt at an infinite but human sacrifice has destroyed those who offered it, I am more in awe of the infinite and eternal sacrifice of our Savior. I think of the magnitude of his suffering, "which suffering caused myself, even God, the greatest of all, to tremble because of pain, and to bleed at every pore, and to suffer both body and spirit" (D&C 19:18). I note also that the herald who is able to bear this suffering the longest is revealed in *Wind and Truth* not to come from noble stock but to be a common man with, we might say, "no form nor comeliness; and when we shall see him, there is no beauty that we should desire him" (Isaiah 53:2).

Besides this portrayal of the reality of infinite suffering, *Wind and Truth* also looks at how the atonement bridges the gap between good intentions and past mistakes. One of my favorite characters in the series is Dalinar, the brother to the king who begins receiving visions of a pending apocalypse. Though the Dalinar we meet in the first two novels is a man trying his best to live up to a strict moral code, he was not always this way. In *Oathbringer*, Sanderson revealed that Dalinar was once a violent warlord, committing all the atrocities associated with pillaging and conquering a kingdom. Though the book ends with Dalinar acknowledging his past crimes and trying to do better, some readers were still disturbed: how could we be asked to empathize with someone who had once burned an entire city of women and children? Latter-day Saint readers might notice resonances with the story of the people of Ammon, which asks the Nephites to forgive and shelter those who have previously made war against them, as the people of Ammon in turn forgive the Lamanites who slaughtered their defenseless husbands and fathers when they repent.

In *Wind and Truth*, this question returns to relevance again as Dalinar experiences a spiritual torment worthy of Alma over his past sins. As he magically relives his past, he questions his worthiness: "He was a different man now, but could anything ever make up for such a terrible thing as he'd done? It was so horrific that seeing it now, he had to acknowledge that any punishment delivered to him would be *just*. He *deserved* it. [...] For all his posturing, his changes in himself didn't restore to life the burned corpses of the children he had killed."* He asks the question that is at the heart of all Christian theology: "Must everything I do have no meaning because of the terrible choices I once made?"† Dalinar is a living embodiment of the question of sin and forgiveness that each person must live with, albeit on a more exaggerated scale than I hope most of us have claim to.

The answer to Dalinar's question comes from a character called Nohadon, a character who Sanderson has confirmed was inspired by King Benjamin.‡ As an ancient king, Nohadon walked among his people and wrote down his wisdom about being a just and virtuous ruler. Now his spirit explains to Dalinar a way out of his impasse. He explains the necessity of mortality and suffering—"The path […] is filled with pain"—but asserts that suffering is necessary for growth—"we are *not* creatures of destinations. It is the journey that shapes us." Nohadon describes the wisdom that comes from repentance through the metaphor of the changes a traveler undergoes on such a journey: "Our callused feet. *Your* callused feet. Our backs strong from carrying the weight of our travels. *Your* back strong from carrying the weight of your travels. Our eyes open. *Your. Eyes. Open.*"§ In this sentence, I hear not only King Benjamin's injunction to live a life of service through work but echoes of the temple endowment, asserting that the fall is necessary to open our eyes so that God's children can grow through experience.

At its heart, Nohadon's explanation of the transformative power of suffering is a Latter-day Saint explanation of the joint power of grace coupled with choice. The atonement provides a scaffolding for moving past our imperfections to become someone better, but it doesn't erase all the wisdom we have gained by going through these experiences.

One of the most repeated mottos in the series is "journey before destination." The way characters

> **Dalinar is a living embodiment of the question of sin and forgiveness.**

---

* Brandon Sanderson, *Wind and Truth* (Tor, 2024), 962.

† Sanderson, *Wind and Truth*, 963.

‡ For this confirmation and more thoughts about how King Benjamin's story interacts with *The Way of Kings*, see Nicholas J. Frederick, "Could Brandon Sanderson Have Saved the Nephites?" *Irreantum* 20, no. 3, 2023. https://irreantum.associationmormonletters.org/_20_3_could-brandon-sanderson-have-saved-the-nephites/

§ Sanderson, *Wind and Truth*, 963.

arrive at the heroic "right action" is so much less important than the experiences that shaped them along the way there. It's this emphasis on the journey—from a Latter-day Saint perspective, we might say "enduring to the end"—that enables Sanderson's writing to be heroic without being didactic. Rather than helping his characters come to a predetermined "correct" conclusion, Sanderson writes them through a path of struggle and shows how their decisions along the path shape them into the people the world needs to save it. It's about the diversity of goodness just as much as it's about the banality of evil.

In many ways, *Wind and Truth* is a novel about a faith crisis. Because it is the midpoint of a ten-book arc, the conclusion to the novel is about the heroes' inadequacy to meet the problems in front of them. There's a disconnect between the characters intentions, the divine help they've been promised, and the results they are seeing around them. This thread can be found in almost every plot line in the book—Dalinar's confrontation with Odium, Szeth's confusion over what is right, Sigzil's ambivalence about his leadership role—but perhaps no plot line is as clearly about a faith crisis as Adolin's defense of Azir. As he defends this city under siege, he

questions why he isn't receiving more divine aid, why he is seemingly left alone when he's doing the right thing. His internal dialogue might sound familiar to anyone who is striving to live the gospel and yet feeling the heavens are silent: "If there were gods, or an Almighty, or something, shouldn't Adolin be getting a little help now and then?"¶

In the first few novels, Adolin unconsciously accepted the religious beliefs he was brought up with as just a part of reality. He automatically bowed his head as his aunt Navani burned a prayer for him before a duel, incorporating it as part of his usual rituals. But by *Wind and Truth*, Adolin has found that this religious worldview can no longer account for his experiences. He is particularly disturbed the problem of theodicy: "Nothing made sense anymore. Adolin felt he was the only one who recognized that the world had gone insane [w]. He wanted the good men whose names he memorized to stop storming *dying*."** Additionally, Adolin seems to struggle with some form of religious scrupulosity, the feeling that he can never live up to the religious ideals his father has asked him to live by. He reflects that he rejected the opportunity to become king of Alethkar because

---

¶ Sanderson, *Wind and Truth*, 747.
** Sanderson, *Wind and Truth*, 1124.

he was afraid of "[e]xpectations versus execution."* He has also grown into an adult who can see the imperfection of the religious people and institutions around him. His father, Dalinar, has become a prophetic figure, we might even say a restorationist prophet who calls out current religious traditions as corrupted echoes of the truth. Yet Adolin is prevented from belief by his knowledge of his father's sins, not only Dalinar's past reputation as a warlord, "the Blackthorn, soaked in blood,"† but the personal actions by which Dalinar has wronged him. In this one character, Sanderson manages to sum up many of the factors that lead good people to struggle with faith.

However, Sanderson doesn't let Adolin take the typical path of moving into secularism. In fact, he mirrors Adolin's faith crisis with a similar faith crisis for the most secular character in the series, Adolin's cousin Jasnah. Jasnah is known as a great scholar and as a heretic who dismisses all supernatural ideas about the universe. She embodies the typical secular hypothesis about religion, believing that everything about it can be explained away: "It strikes me that religion—in its essence—seeks to take natural events and ascribe supernatural causes to them. I, however, seek to take supernatural events and find the natural meanings behind them."‡ She sets rationalism and religion as "opposite sides of a card"; as rationalism increases, religiosity must correspondingly decrease.

In *Wind and Truth*, Jasnah's secular moral compass is put to the test in a high-stakes battle of wits that she ultimately loses. This point shocked many readers who were unconvinced by this dismantling of Jasnah's point of view.§ Perhaps this is due to Sanderson's limitations as a writer: it's hard to construct a philosophical debate between geniuses unless one is in fact a philosopher and a genius, which not many novelists are. However, I personally think much of the controversy is the result of Sanderson digging at the roots of readers' belief in secularism as a neutral perspective, a "view from nowhere,"¶ rather than an ideology with its own limitations. This failure plants the series firmly into a postsecular world, a world

---

* Sanderson, *Wind and Truth*, 521.

† Sanderson, *Wind and Truth*, 1124.

‡ Brandon Sanderson, *The Way of Kings* (Tor, 2010), 1093.

§ For examples of the fan discussion around this scene, see this forum thread on Sanderson's official fan site: https://www.17thshard.com/forums/topic/198470-why-so-much-hate-on-the-debate/

¶ Branch, Lori Peterson. "Postsecular Studies," *The Routledge Companion to Literature and Religion* (Routledge, 2016), 95.

that cannot assume the triumph of science over religion but must accept both as important parts of the human experience. Of all the characters over the five-book arc who undergo faith crises, Jasnah is perhaps the one who experiences the most violent break: "realizing that she might have built the bedrock of her life upon a flawed philosophy that even she didn't truly believe, shook her to her core."** As Jasnah

> **By setting aside whether religion is true or not, Sanderson is able to ask questions about what it is like.**

says as she contemplates her failure, "she'd spent her life spurning the existence of deity—and had now been bested by one."†† I suspect this loss is Sanderson's way of setting Jasnah up to become more open in future books to ways of knowing that are, if not outright religious, then at least less secular.

These two mirrored faith crises— Adolin's crisis of faith and Jasnah's

crisis of secularism—illustrate the power that *Wind and Truth* has to really get at the heart of what it means to be a religious person. The novel accepts no easy answers, either from religion or from its detractors. Instead, the wide proliferation of characters and perspectives (something that can be exasperating about fantasy epics) allows Sanderson to explore a mosaic of human relationships to the divine without committing to a specific confession of faith. By setting aside whether religion is true or not, Sanderson is able to ask questions about what it is *like*:

What is it like to gradually become aware of your religion's flawed history?

What is it like when your faith and your identity seem to clash?

What is it like when you suddenly realize that there's more to the world than your previous conceptions?

What is it like to rebuild yourself after religious abuse?

What is it like when someone you care about is leaving the faith that you love?

What is it like to let go of control and accept God's will?

The power that I see in *Wind and Truth*, and in the Stormlight Archive overall, is the power to build out this landscape of religious varieties. There are, of course, many ways to build

---

** Sanderson, *Wind and Truth*, 1125.

††   Sanderson, *Wind and Truth*, 1124.

this sort of understanding, though fiction has proven time and again its strength at building empathy, at causing us to experience faith through someone else's experience. I have only scratched the surface here of the religious questions that Sanderson attempts to portray.* The fact is that this book is jam-packed with myriad examples of the way religious people experience life. In spite of what may be regarded as its flaws, I think that, over time, readers will come to see this book as a crucial part of the overall arc of the series' message about what it means to be a human: to be a spiritual being having a mortal experience.

*A whole article about religion in *Wind and Truth* that barely mentions Szeth's quest to purify his homeland? Clearly, there is more to be written.

LIZ BUSBY is a writer and scholar interested in the intersection between religion and science fiction/fantasy. Her writing has been published in *BYU Studies, Wayfare Magazine, The Journal of the Fantastic in the Arts,* and *SFRA Review.* She teaches writing at BYU and co-hosts the podcast *The Storming Journey,* which reads the Stormlight Archive as a sacred text. Follow her writing on www.lizbusby.com.

Fiction

Young Hagoth Plays It Safe

Theric Jepson

Jarom was old. His skin was tight rather than wrinkled and the sunbeams from the window caught his long white beard as he entered the room. His robe was a simple brown, but embroidered with enough detail to make it expensive. He cleared his throat and leaned against a stool as he looked over them. His voice was strong but scratched, as if he had let a cat play with it before joining the boys as they sat on short stools intended for much younger students.

"My dear boys about to become men," he said, fixing them all with eyes that seemed to jump around the room like frying bacon, "because manhood follows boyhood as surely as boyhood precedes manhood, it is necessary that you, being boys, and thus men-to-be, must prepare to be the men you will become before you cease to be the boys you are now—it is good to see your smiling faces. Before becoming men—while you are still boys—it is incumbent upon you, and incumbent upon me as your teacher, and incumbent upon our society—as it requires men—to decide and embark upon your path of manhoodian labors, in which you will spend the rest of your days, and to do so in a sensible manner with the proper instruction and opportunities for observation and so forth. And so, in these coming months, you will be given opportunity to meet with and visit with and talk with and sit with and listen to and so forth, under all the men in this great city, even Zarahemla, whom this year are seeking boys to become men under their tutelage as apprentices of their craft, that their superiority of skill and knowledge may pass fully unto you, the new generation, that things will come to be as great or even greater than they are now."

Jarom paused, pulled from somewhere within his stool a finely carved wooden mug, took a sip of water, then brushed down his beard before continuing. "But that is not all of course. It is well enough to learn to be a man from another man—or other men, as in the case of an apprenticeship in leading warriors into battle, or in dungmongering, an occupation often underappreciated by those who just get their food at market and never think about where it actually comes from. But also you must learn to be a man from yourself. For a man should not be any man, a man should be his own man, the only man that a man can be, at least fully, you understand." Jarom frowned and looked sternly at them, as if he were worried they might willfully misunderstand him. "And so you will plot your future with care and ambition and so forth. Your opportunities are grand this year. Enom the silversmith is looking to take on up to two apprentices. Importers and tailors are looking for apprentices. Of course, as always, half a dozen lawyers or so. And the highlight this year, great Mulek, son of Amaron of the great house of armorers, making the greatest

armor this nation or any nation has ever known, and all the great things they've done for us keeping people alive and so forth. Of course," and here he chuckled, "you'll have to beat our young Hagoth for that position, so . . . heh. Anyway."

All the other rich men's boys looked over at Hagoth who looked at his hands and tried to think of something other than his father, armor, or the gas he was struggling to keep inside his body. Why hadn't anyone reminded him that drinking goat's milk for breakfast gave him the poots?

"Today we will start by visiting Mikal, who leads the temple guardians, then Boron whose imports allow our best men to look their finest. And, speaking of clothes, we'll see someone who makes them, someone who sells them and," he chuckled, "the local boatmaker."

Hagoth had no idea Zarahemla still had a boatmaker. His father Mulek hadn't made fun of him in months and besides, what did Zarahemla really need a boatmaker for, anyway? Hagoth had only been to the sea—and on a boat—once, in Morianton, when he was three, before his mother died. It was his first memory—and the only one of her. She was telling his father to shut up. He treasured that memory. Boats were great. But in Zarahemla?

Boron, for instance, didn't use boats. He didn't even "import." Basically he snuck into Lamanite lands, killed birds, then sold their feathers. "It's exciting, it's dangerous, it's profitable, and you can always keep a feather for yourself. No better way to impress the ladies. You're all old enough to know what really matters."

All the potential masters, like Boron, met them dressed in their best finery until the boatmaker, Lehonti, who came to his shop door dressed in a holey sackcloth tunic and worn woolen pants—reminding them that no matter what the clothing hawker had said, wool was not traditional finery.

The boatmaker sneezed, spraying tobacco juice all over Jarom's young charges. "Sorry," he mumbled. "Bit of a cold." He wiped his nose on his forearm, leaving a trail of snot in the hair that glistened in the afternoon sun like a small army of slugs. "So," he slurred. "Boats." He nodded and slapped the doorway to his shop. "Let's go in."

The shop was dark and smelled of dust and tar and rotted fruit and that unpleasant mix of regret and desperation usually only present at public executions.

Lehonti stopped in front of a tiny, half-formed boat. "This is the best we can do around here. River's too shallow for anything worthwhile."

He belched in a way disrespectful to the music of the sea. "Sorry," he

Ill: Maddie Baker

said to Jarom. "Been a rough week. Bad year. Lousy career." He laughed then turned to Jarom's students. "Which is why I'm gonna try extra hard to convince one of you to apprentice with me this year: I need new ideas and I don't have an heir."

The truth, as Hagoth well knew for his father often spoke of it, was that every girl Lehonti had ever liked, Mulek had wooed away with trinkets and baubles and all for a laugh at Lehonti's expense. His father had also, famously, punched Lehonti once after Lehonti got betrothed. And then Mulek had married Lehonti's betrothed. Who became Hagoth's mother.

Lehonti collapsed onto a sawdusty bench and sneezed at them again. "Look at you," he said and they did look at each other, wondering who might smell badly enough to end up here. "In a few months you'll put on those fancy presentations and talk about your big plans. Then you'll all get apprenticed and start doing a job and never think about your big plans again. And neither will nobody else. Jarom don't remember mine, do you?"

Jarom was silent and dignified as he brushed a bit of sawdust from his robe, then, when it caught an updraft into his face, frantically waved it away.

"Yeah. I was gonna turn this city into a major river port. As if the water here'd ever be deep enough for anything bigger than that bit of dung sitting half-made over there." He belched again. "Excuse me. I need to medicate. Any questions about boats?"

Hagoth had several. A port? Where would ships go? To the sea? Was it true that on the sea people still moved more stuff than just fishing tackle—like in the old days of Father Lehi? Was it possible to go far from the shore? Was it true anyone who did, who left the Promised Land, was cursed? Are you still mad about all those girls my father stole from you? What was my mother like? But before he knew which to start with, Lehonti saw him and spat on the ground.

"Mulek's kid." It wasn't a question. "I'm sure your big plans'll stick. Just like your dad's did, and his dad's. You'll be prancing around in your finery soon enough. Already are, from the looks of it. So. Kid. How you gonna save us? I bet you're making armor won't nobody die."

"I—" Hagoth knew the right answer. His father had already written out his goal for him, even though Hagoth wasn't even supposed to start deciding on a field for another two months. He would say, "I, Hagoth, son of Mulek the son of Amaron and heir of a great tradition of saving the lives of our nation's noblest warriors, do hereby declare my intention that should another war ever arise—which thing I dearly hope not—I shall reinvent the great contributions of my forebears and craft an armor stronger and safer and lighter than any before. I will begin by investigating means to better flexibility in breastplates by improving upon the layering technique invented by my father." And as his father had already perfected that improvement for him, about eighteen months later Hagoth would be paraded in Zarahemla as a prodigy, an already accomplished genius, and the money would start rolling in all over again.

about in his finery. Course, if'n my original plan to persuade us all 'to become an aquatic nation, trading with our neighbors upon holy waters' suddenly happens, then suuuure. But I failed. Obviously. And so will alla you. 'Cept for Mulek's kid cause nothing never goes wrong for them."

Almost as if these were the words Jarom had been waiting for, he said, "Thank you, Lehonti. Always a pleasure. This way, boys."

They filed out behind him, but Hagoth lingered. He wanted to touch

Hagoth knew the right answer. His father had already written out his goal for him.

Which was all well and good except Hagoth was pretty sure he would never repeat that first success. After one fake success it would be pure failure from then on out. Hagoth had embarrassed himself more than once by failing to fasten his robes or tunic properly before leaving home in the morning. The idea of actually designing clothes—let alone ones meant to keep people alive—he couldn't quite imagine it, destiny or no.

"…but given most fishermen and ferriers just build and maintain their own boats, it's not like you'll ever see a Zarahemla boatmaker parading

the half-formed shell, run his hand along its curved wood.

Lehonti staggered over to him, taking a bag of wine from the shelf on his way. "Hey."

"Yes?"

Lehonti looked in Hagoth's face for a moment, then turned away to rub a circle into the dirt with the toe of his sandle. "So. Um. Tell your father that I, uh, hear some nations fight their battles on water? And, so, uh, I'm looking for a partner? Making war boats or something?"

Hagoth nodded. His father hated boats. And the sea, for that matter. And Lehonti.

"Okay. But I'm not sure—"

Lehonti's eyes snapped back onto Hagoth's. "Just tell your brotherslaying father, okay? It won't kill ya!"

"Okay. I will." And Hagoth ran away without any of the grace of that boat in Morianton which had borne him along.

###

"So," Mulek said as he ripped the turkey meat from the bone. "Who'd you go see on your first day?"

"Um, some kind of fabric maker, a clothing merchant, a feather importer, a temple guardian, and, um, and, a boatmaker."

"What? Not Lehonti!"

"Yes, sir."

"I can't believe Jarom took you to see that brotherslayer. Like he needs an apprentice. So how's the old drunk doing?"

"He's, uh, drunk."

Mulek laughed loudly and appreciatively, spitting wine down the front of his tunic. Not that it mattered. He could afford more and finer.

"He, uh, he said in some places wars are fought on boats. He wondered if you'd be interested."

Mulek curled his lip. "Stupid as ever. Shame I'm too respectable to dump him in the wastepits anymore."

"But—it's not—boats aren't too bad, right? It's just—Lehonti you don't like."

Mulek shrugged. "What's the difference. Maybe there are people somewhere who live on water, but not Nephites. Nephi only built a boat to get here. And now we're here! Any fool who would chase the water would be laughed at for three generations. Like they say, God made fish and God made Nephites, but he did not make Nephites fish."

"What?"

"Three generations! Lehonti's proof of this. Now even his soul floats!" Mulek laughed at his own joke, but Hagoth had never understood why it wouldn't be better for a soul to float. Who wants to sink?

"We're sinking," cries the boat-running assistant. *"We will die!"*

Hagoth however stands stern, watching his boat fill with water. "We didn't come into the ocean this far just to sink. Think of your soul!"

Ill: *Maddie Baker*

"My soul doesn't float! What, are you crazy?"

"You're on the sea now!" declares Hagoth. "It had better float."

"When are you coming to see me?"

Hagoth shook his head. "I don't know. Jarom hasn't told you?"

"No." His father pushed aside the rest of the turkey carcass. "Take that to the dogs and send a runner to Jarom. Tell him to come tomorrow. I'll get the taste of that brotherslayer out of your mouths."

###

Hagoth stood with his father and Jarom as the other boys watched and waited and tried to listen. Jarom was wearing a new and vibrantly blue wool tunic he had been given yesterday by the merchant, and a crown of brightly colored feathers from the importer.

"Yes, they're very nice," Mulek said to Jarom, "but you don't need armor and we both know I can get whatever apprentice I want. Sit down and listen with the boys."

Jarom furrowed his brow, kicked at the floor, and walked to a corner to pout behind his beard, reaching up occasionally to finger his feathers.

"Now you all know what you're doing," said Mulek in his booming voice, walking over to the boys as Hagoth tried to skip around him so he could sit down and be normal. "You're all supposed to figure out how to improve our city and the world. And you probably also know that most people never actually do that. But seriously, what good can a single potter or weaver actually do in their life? But armorers? We are different. When my father Amaron invented the modern breastplate we immediately saw a drop in casualties. And my goal was to improve upon his improvements. Many of you were sired because I kept your fathers alive. And thanks to that prick Moroni—"

"Hey!"

"Oh. Little Moronihah. Didn't see you there. Tell your father I said hi. But as I was saying, thanks to that prick Moroni, my designs were forced to be shared among all the cities' armorers, which was of course, in the end, an enlightened decision—tell him I said so, kid—that saved many lives."

And made his father a lot of money, as Hagoth well knew. His father, being his father, had found a way to earn a portion from every breastplate every one of those armorers ever made.

"So it is possible, at the end of this process, to make a goal that will change the nation. And I guarantee you that whoever is selected to be my apprentice, I will do all I can to assure their success at meeting their goal."

"Yes, Hagoth, sir. A new land! You found it! You found it! You met your goal!"

Hagoth nodded. Of course he had. What doubt had there ever been?

His father gave all the boys a single shinguard. As they left the armory, they broke sticks off the tree Hagoth's mother had planted and started hitting each other.

###

Hagoth had exited the butcher's to throw up—so now he was behind the rest of the boys. He scanned the knoll. The twins were hiding in the shadows of a heavily vined tree at the edge of a garden; he walked over to join them.

"Hi, Hagoth."

"Hi, Mahujah."

"Hi, world-changing-armormaker."

"Shut up, Mahijah."

Mahijah and Mahujah laughed. "What's for lunch?"

Hagoth sat down across from them. "Just some jerky and a corn patty."

Mahijah slapped his forehead in shock. "Curelom jerky? Wow!"

"It's not curelom. Curelom's too expensive to just turn it into jerky."

"All the more reason for your dad to do it."

Hagoth couldn't argue with that, so instead he said, "You can't even get curelom anymore." He bit into his patty.

Mahujah burped. "What does curelom taste like, anyway?"

"Just like, you know, like turkey. They're almost the same."

Both twins choked. "Turkey? Why would anyone spend that much on turkey?"

Hagoth rolled his eyes. "My father."

"What, does he even vomit money now? Is that what you were doing?"

"No." Hagoth chewed and swallowed. "But even though I threw up, that was awesome when he flipped the goat's heart out through its throat."

"Yes!" Mahijah jumped up to mime the action. "Let's be butchers!"

The twins, no surprise, wanted to go into business together but the butcher was only looking for one apprentice. The only masters looking for two apprentices this year were the silversmith, the loom guy, and the manager of the city's walls.

"No way we're doing the walls."

"No way," agreed Mahujah. "And wool was never considered fine apparel before last year, so that's not going to last."

"But that might make it the perfect choice," argued Mahijah. "We could

"A new land! You found it! You met your goal!" Hagoth nodded. Of course he had. What doubt had there ever been?

make it permanently fashionable! Then wool's value will go up and we could make real money!"

"Nah," said Hagoth. "It won't last. Who wants to wear wool in the summer? That guy's a dope if he really thinks he needs two apprentices. Want some jerky?"

He held it out to them but they waved it away.

"Oh no. I'm much too poor to eat *curelom*."

"It's not curelom."

"Hey!" One twin punched the other. "We could farm cureloms!"

Hagoth rolled his eyes. "First you have to find one."

Mahujah giggled. "You need two."

Mahijah smirked. "Looks like Hagoth won't be getting that baby-making apprenticeship."

"What do you mean, no one on board knows how to make babies?" Hagoth yells at his assistant. "How will we people the new land!"

But that was too silly even for him.

Mulek smeared the boar grease from his chin across his cheek as he led the men around the table in laughter. "Good one, Levi! Ha! That'd show him! But seriously, Moroni's definitely going to be checking every city looking for the cheapest price on breastplates. We can't let him break us."

"Like he did his nose!" yelled Levi, and they all laughed again.

Hagoth sat in his corner with his plate of boar and lentils, and drifted away.

Moroni is with his army on the seashore, trapped by the Lamanite hordes with his back to the sea. "Whadllwedo?" whimpers his lieutenant. But Moroni stands stoically, staring out to sea, his crooked nose casting a shadow on the sparkling waves in the fading light or possibly the growing light depending on where—the sea's to the west, right? so where's that put his nose?—anyway, in the fading light. He closes his eyes briefly and decides to do his faith thing and says "God will save us" and at that moment a sail appears on the horizon and Moroni's war face cracks momentarily as he whispers, "God—or Hagoth?"

"Hagoth!"

Hagoth jumped, sending his plate and himself to the floor. ("Like the leather market," joked Levi and all the men, once again, laughed.) Hagoth stood and brushed himself off. "Yes, father?"

"Omner's leaving for Morianton tonight. Carry his bags to the gate."

"Yes, father."

Mulek stood and clasped arms with Omner, commending him for being the most profitable of them all this past year. Hagoth scrambled to find Omner's bags, but not before

Omner joined him and pointed to the proper ones. They were heavy, but as Omner and Hagoth walked from the house, Hagoth still found the breath to ask him about the sea. "Do you ever go out on the boats?"

"What? No. Do I look like a fisherman?"

"But you've seen the sea beasts?"

"A time or two. But until we have fishermen brave enough to slay them, what do I care? Besides, watching the sea is for simpletons and zealots. I'm a man of business. Like your father."

Hagoth tried to think of a question to follow that. Omner laughed at his scrunched-up face.

"I'll tell you one story of the sea, though."

"Yes?"

"When I was a boy, a man and his boat crashed upon our shore. His hair was darker than even a Lamanite's, though his skin was much like our own. He was not well—nearly dead from the lack of fresh water. On his boat, we found devices of curious workmanship. He spoke no language known to our scholars, and died before he could learn ours, and so we know not what land he came from, what goals he had, or the purposes of the devices he carried. Nor could we recreate their manner of craft. But we still have those devices. His boat we burned in honor of his journey."

"Wow. So—do you think he was from Jerusalem?"

"No, no. Wrong sea."

"Wrong sea?"

"Across Lamanite lands there is a second sea—the sea our fathers travelled, if you believe the stories."

"You have boatmakers in Morianton?"

"Of course, a few. Fishermen must fish. And marlin is the curelom of the sea. But there is danger in going out that far."

"Then why do they do it?"

"Because men like me will pay for it. We can afford to lose a few fishermen for the occasional marlin. When you're an apprentice, come see me. I will feed you marlin."

"Thank you."

"Ah, Hagoth. Not marlin again!"

Hagoth looked across the table at his assistant. "Land-livers would kill for this meal, yet you complain. Have you no shame?"

"I'm sorry. I'm a fool."

"That's right you are."

Hagoth watched Omner pass through the gates, then turned toward home. He kicked rocks out of the street and let his mind wander. When he looked up, he'd missed a turn in the darkness. He was no longer on the broad path home, but in a narrow path. The buildings tilted slightly and he could see few stars. Once he realized where he was, he wondered *why* he was. Just around this corner was Lehonti's place. Surely this time of night the man would be gone—perhaps Hagoth could slip in and touch the boat he was building? It was worth a try.

He walked quietly. Just before the entrance, he beheld a man fallen to the earth and drunken with wine. Lehonti.

Hagoth listened to him snore. Nothing other than Lehonti's naked legs were between him and the entrance. He stepped over them. He ran his fingers along the body of the boat. He placed his ear against it, almost as if the sound of the ocean might be trapped inside. But he'd taken enough chances. He walked back to the entrance—where Lehonti's hand struck him like a snake, grabbing on and pulling him to the ground.

"What're y'doing here, boy?"

Lehonti's eyes were more red than white. The skin of his face black and mottled in the starlight. Lehonti's

Ill: Maddie Baker

breath was stronger than even his father's, but also rotten in a way his father's never was. His expression changed as he recognized Hagoth. "You." An idea floated across his rheumy eyes. "He'd never know wha' happened t'you . . . ."

"No, sir, please—I just wanted to see your boat."

"The des'lation y'did." Lehonti tried to stand but his movements were as slurred as his words. "Y're here to steal sumpn'r break sumpn." He fell back to the floor, blocking Hagoth's escape.

"No, I just—! I went on a boat with my mother when I was little and—"

"Y'r mother!" Lehonti burst into huge sobs. He flung his face on the ground. Hagoth was stunned. He'd never seen a grown man weep before—not even one as drunk as Lehonti.

"Sir?"

"Course y're her kid. Course. I knew it. I just . . . ."

Lehonti sat back up, sort of up, then pulled his tunic up to wipe his face, revealing a bulging stomach that protected his modesty. "Y'like boats, d'you?"

"Yes, sir. I— They're all I— Yes, sir."

Lehonti nodded and seemed to fall asleep before grasping onto the doorway and pulling himself up. "I'll show you some stuff."

Hagoth wasn't about to say no. But he did wonder if Lehonti would remember any of this. And if so, who he might tell.

###

Only a week left of visits, Jarom reminded the students as they went into the brewer's. The brewer had laid out mugs of different beers for their inspection. Most of the boys crowded around, learning about a brewer's life. The more religious kids hung back, and Hagoth stayed with them. He hated the smell of beer. Much better the smell of the sea. He couldn't really remember that smell, but no doubt it was lovely.

In fact, the sea smelled like . . . fish tacos . . . only . . . less spicy. Like the cook had added too much salt and not enough chili peppers. The salty fish-taco air sprayed foam like beer upon the top of the boat where brave Hagoth stood, his hands on his hips. He had been upon the sea for a month or two or however long it takes to get far enough from land to make it all disappear and look like there's only water in the world. That far. Hagoth was searching for a new land. And he would find one. Perhaps he would have to contend with giants or with . . . giant spiders or . . . giant mushrooms—with claws!—but he would find a new land. And when he found that new land he would

"Hagoth!"

"Uh? What? Yes?" Hagoth checked the corner of his mouth for drool as a beer-soaked towel smacked him across the face. He pulled it off and looked around. He was alone in the brewery. The brewer laughed at him and pointed to the door, where echoes of the twins' laughter trickled through. Hagoth wiped his face on his sleeve and hurried after them.

###

Hagoth stood looking at his father. "About the goal presentations."

"You have yours memorized?"

"Yes, but—"

"Good, good. Go practice some more. Work on inflection."

"But I—"

"If you want to add something about leather ties or even metal clasps, go ahead. I figure we can charge another senum-per without rebellion and they won't cost us even close to that."

"Okay."

Hagoth watches his feet as he walks to the back part of the boat.

"What is wrong?" His assistant looks at him with worried eyes. "Is it the waves?"

"No, no." He straightens his shoulders. "I am a man of the sea. And we men of the sea make our own destiny."

Hagoth looked out a window at the setting sun. Men of destiny have places to go, after all.

###

The clothmaker had a loud generous laugh that quaked his belly and filled the room. "C'mon! You all know it! That smell! It's piss!" He laughed again. "Maybe I'll have you all donate to the vat before you go."

"I am a man of the sea. And we men of the sea make our own destiny."

The boys all laughed and elbowed each other even as their faces paled.

"Oh, come now. Take that green tunic." He pointed at Hagoth. "I'm the only man in the land what can make that shade. And no, I won't tell you how to do it at home. Well, maybe one of you—in a couple weeks—am I right? Am I right? But I will tell you how to make the color stick to the cloth. And that's with piss. Soak it in piss."

All the boys pointed at Hagoth's tunic and giggled.

"Yes," he said to his crew. "Yes, the sea can smell like piss sometimes, but that's why it's so good at making virtue stick to your soul. The sea makes good men better and better men great. Take my tunic for example . . . ."

The parents and masters and a few priests squatted on the low stools meant for children—those who met in Jarom's classroom the other months of the year. They looked like they were playing peekaboo from behind their knees. Based on the number of those gathered today wearing wool, even in the heat and humidity, Hagoth thought the twins may have made the right decision. He was with the rest of the boys, leaning against the walls at the back of the room.

As Jarom entered the room, the silversmith stood and walked to him. His forearms were wrapped in silver snakes; his fingers coated with rings and thimbles, his ears and nose decorated enough to make them stretch; the headdress he wore shot silver sunrays into the air above him, with small silver birds and angels hanging from them making a tinkling sound as he held Jarom's arms and spoke to him. The two men laughed as they pointed at some of the boys. Before returning to his seat, the silversmith removed the sun from his head and handed it to Jarom, who shook slightly as he took it and placed it on his own head, smashing the three feathercrowns he already wore there.

Jarom stood and nodded solemnly at those assembled as they looked at him from above their knees.

"Yes, hello, hello," he said. "Today is that day which all boys wait for while they are boys, until the day they become men, because that day is the day they no longer need to wait for, it is the day they cease to be boys and become men. Today is the day they announce their plans for improving our society and—"

The crowd started clapping, which startled Jarom, but when they didn't stop he smiled and waved at the crowd and then gestured for the first boy to come up.

One by one, Hagoth's peers stood and gave their spiels, lofty goals doomed to failure. No matter how cleverly you plan to cut them up, a butcher cannot return curelom to the forests. No matter how much you want to make finery finer, if silver can't be made into thread, it can't be made into thread.

"Hagoth?"

"Yes?"

"What are you thinking?"

Hagoth sighs and looks deep into the sea. Hundreds of feet below him, the beasts engaged in their ageless dances. "I was thinking how few of the boys I grew up with were able to predict how plain their lives would actually be."

"Oh." Silence. "What was your goal?"

"Oh, just *'to conquer the seas and discover new lands and bring wealth and honor and glory of an entirely new sort to my father and my city and my nation.' I had memorized it perfectly. I had practiced it. I was to 'ride the waves of fortune' and 'feel the soul of mother water in my feet' and all sorts of things. And look. Here I am. The exception. The rare success."*

"And now Hagoth, son of Mulek, son of Amaron, will present his decision and request, and then I will present him to his new master. Wonder who that might be?" Jarom chuckled along with the crowd.

Hagoth walked to the front and stood looking over. His father's stern face, the twins' happiness at being in wool, the priests trying to hold their robes together with their knees poking into the air. Back in the corner, by the door, an ill-dressed boatmaker leaned against a wall. He raised an eyebrow at Hagoth then turned his face.

"I, Hagoth, son of Mulek the son of Amaron and heir of a great tradition of saving the lives of our nation's noblest warriors, do hereby declare my intention that—"

Everyone held their breath.

"Only you can save us, Hagoth!"

The sea beast crawled onto the ship, the rain and wind whipping his many lips, revealing jaws filled with thousands of needle teeth. The beast snapped. Hagoth strapped on his father's armor and walked forward. It would not do to fail.

"—my intention that—should another war ever arise—which thing I dearly hope not—I shall reinvent the great contributions of my forebears and craft an armor stronger and safer and lighter than any before.

I will begin by investigating means to better flexibility in breastplates by improving upon the layering technique invented by my father."

Everyone clapped and Mulek leapt to the stage and, wearing an atypical smile, slapped an arm around his son.

Hagoth smiled back. After all—maybe he would fail.

THERIC JEPSON is the editor of *Irreantum* and the author of *Just Julie's Fine*. He has the expected number of fingers per hand.

MADDIE BAKER is an illustrator and comic maker from Idaho. She recently graduated from the Sam Fox School's Illustration and Visual Culture MFA. She loves cannellini beans, Jane Austen, and working with analog media. Her work is about the beauty and humor of everyday life, especially as it is found in women's stories and scripture.

Poetry

RENTED ROOM

JS ABSHER

The window glass has rippled
a century of moons.
It does not see out clearly
nor clearly show the room—

a pine table, a wooden chair
pushed under the table; the far
dingy drywall where Jesus
kneels in a calendar,

his fingers tightly interlaced;
a woman holding a letter
who's trying to write I'm sorry
but failing over and over.

She steps to the window
where she brushes away flies—
dead how many years? Watery
panes hide watery eyes.

While Jesus gazes at the ceiling,
her glance strays outside. Dusk
and drizzle make it hard to see out
far, harder to escape the face

that looks back from the glass.
She turns from the dark world,
clicks on the stereo, her one
nice thing. Rien de rien, the bird

in a cedar hears, je ne regrette rien,
I paid it all, swept it away—
whatever they did to me, to me ...
She lifts the needle and sways

to her inner tremolo. Her lamp
glows through the blinds and cedars
toward Jesus pacing the starry sky
and swatting away prayers.

Originally published in Visions International, *issue 95 (2017).*

JS ABSHER has published two full-length books of poetry—*Skating Rough Ground* (Kelsay Press, 2022) and *Mouth Work* (St. Andrews University Press, 2016), winner of the Lena Shull Award from the North Carolina Poetry Society. Absher's poems have won awards from *BYU Studies Quarterly* and *Dialogue*, and have been nominated for the Pushcart Prize and the Best of the Net. His poems have been published by *NC Literary Review, Triggerfish Critical Review, Tar River Poetry, The McNeese Review, Irreantum, Wayfare,* and others. Absher lives in Raleigh, NC, with his wife, Patti.

Fiction

Music of the Spirit

Annaliese Lemmon

When my primary teachers told me that the Holy Ghost spoke as a still, small voice or a burning in the bosom, I was always confused. Since the day I was confirmed, I experienced the Spirit as music—a soundtrack constantly playing to fit whatever circumstances I'm in. A quick-paced brassy theme to warn of danger. A high flute trill to accompany an epiphany. Once, when I despaired at a tough AP World History essay question, the final boss theme from a video game played in my mind. A boss that had taken me days to conquer. I sat for a moment, gathering the resolve I'd used in my many attempts, then tackled the question. I happily received a B+.

No one else can hear this soundtrack. That is, until test day in Spanish 3. I'd confidently turned in my unit one test with five minutes to spare and was packing up my binder. My classmates chatted in a low hum as we waited for the bell to dismiss us—except for Robin, seated in the next row over. They rarely spoke outside of conversation practice, but this time, they leaned over the bar anchoring their chair to the desk and whispered to

me. "Do you have to play a fanfare whenever you turn in a test?"

A record scratched through my mind and I nearly dropped my binder. "You heard that?" I hadn't been humming along with it, had I?

Robin raised their eyebrow with a silver piercing. "Kinda hard to miss."

"I'm sorry." My cheeks burned. I must have been humming. The theme song from *Pink Panther* started to run through my head, though in a lower register than the usual tenor sax. What that was supposed to mean, I had no clue.

"Is that 'Pink Panther' on the tuba?"

I just stared in answer. Robin played tuba in band. Of course they'd recognize that instrument.

"Look, you may have accommodations, but headphones will keep you from being distracting." The bell rang and they shot out the door without waiting for a reply.

This was definitely not me humming.

My immediate thought was that I needed to tell Allison. I'd known her since Sunbeams, and she'd been the first person I'd told about the music.

At lunch I headed to her table by the exit for the hot food line. All the seats were taken by her basketball teammates. I stood to Allison's right, shifting awkwardly from foot to foot as people brushed past. Allison

didn't look my way, even when I cleared my throat.

This wasn't working. I didn't want to explain things in front of her friends, either. I went back to my usual, much-emptier spot against the far wall and texted Allison, *Can we talk?* No reply came as I chewed my way through my peanut butter and jelly sandwich. A single flute played in my mind—my part of a "Greensleeves" duet I had once performed with Allison. The song sounded empty without the second part that would probably never play with it again. Allison had given up flute for basketball when high school started.

At least Heavenly Father understood my loneliness, though He had yet to answer my prayers for a new friend. Allison was tall and athletic, with perfectly behaved blonde hair. Of course she made new friends easily. I, on the other hand, was short and fat, with dark curls that frizzed everywhere. Few people cared to talk to me.

By the end of the day, Allison still hadn't texted back. However, she could no longer avoid me, as she was my ride home. But if she couldn't even spare the courtesy of an acknowledgment, I wasn't sure I *wanted* to talk to her. I silently slid into the passenger seat of her ten-year-old silver sedan.

Allison smiled as she started the car. "Hey, Baylee, what's going on?"

I shrugged.

"You said you wanted to talk?"

I folded my arms in on myself. "Pink Panther" on the tuba started playing in my mind again. What was that supposed to mean? The song was associated with mystery or searching for something. Did Heavenly Father want me to get some clues by talking with Allison? Fine. I looked down and fiddled with the strings of my hoodie. "Someone told me they could hear the music in my mind."

Allison glanced at me with wide eyes. "You still hear that?"

The "Pink Panther" faded into cold silence. Of all the things she could have said . . . "Why wouldn't I?"

"Well, you haven't mentioned it in a while."

When would we have the chance to talk about it anymore? I barely saw her outside carpool and church. "Forget it." Guess I'd misinterpreted that song.

"No, tell me. Who is it? Is it a boy?" She grinned.

I stared out at the large yellowing trees that shaded the roads everywhere in Oregon. "It's Robin Hermsen."

"Oh." Allison's smile faded. "I didn't know you were friends with . . . them."

"I'm not. At least . . ." I bit my lip. Bringing this up felt more and more like a bad idea, but Allison still knew how to talk to people better than I did. "What do you think I should do?"

"How much have you said?"

"Nothing, really. They think the music came from my phone."

"Maybe it's better that way. Robin doesn't go to church. They don't know about the Spirit. You don't want people to think you're crazy."

"Maybe." After seeing how confused our teachers had been at this manifestation of the Spirit, we had agreed it was better to keep it to ourselves. But my stomach felt heavy at the thought. Shouldn't it be different when someone else heard the same thing? Wasn't I supposed to be a missionary and explain the Holy Ghost? And what if Robin thought they were crazy when they realized nobody else could hear the music? They deserved some answers, didn't they?

And maybe this was the answer to my prayer for a new friend. I closed my eyes. *Heavenly Father, do you want me to explain everything to Robin?*

An upbeat song from an RPG played in my mind, from a scene where the group pledges that they will stick together, no matter that one of them is a clone of the demonic villain. That sounded like a yes. But I didn't feel the happiness or warmth that was supposed to come with a positive answer from the Spirit. Instead, my chest felt tight. *How do I say it?* The only answer I got was the RPG song continuing on loop as we finished our three-mile drive in silence.

###

The next day at lunch, I stood in the corner of the cafeteria near the entrance, searching for Robin. Mozart's "Flute Concerto No. 2" danced through my mind, a piece that usually relaxed me. But this time, it did nothing to calm my racing heart. How could I explain the Holy Ghost to someone who didn't know the gospel? What if I said something stupid? What if Robin didn't like me?

Finally, I spotted them at a table against the wall opposite of where I usually sat. As I hoped, they were alone. I'd never noticed them hanging out with anyone, though admittedly, I'd never paid them much attention before. Did the whole school ignore them like I had? Or worse? I'd heard the things some said about trans people, and I knew the suicide statistics for them were not good. Maybe Heavenly Father had let them listen to my music because they needed a friend as much as I did. As if in response, the peaceful Mozart played a bit louder in my mind. I must be thinking on the right track.

Unfortunately, Robin sat hunched over a salad while watching their phone, wearing black headphones that disappeared into their short black hair. Their black backpack sat next to them, the attached chains and miniature plastic skulls sprawling all over the table. They may as well have been wearing a sign that said "DO NOT DISTURB ON PAIN OF DEATH." I gripped my backpack straps tight. Maybe another time would be better. But when? There might not be enough time before class. Also, people would be likely to overhear. At least in the cafeteria, there was enough ambient noise to give us some privacy.

Mozart's music continued. God always prepared the way, right? I took a deep breath and walked over. I leaned over the table to try to catch their eye. They glanced at me, then slid their backpack to the floor without a word.

Well, that was easy. I set my lunchbag on the table where the backpack had been, then pulled out the bag of cookies I'd made the night before. No one could say no to chocolate chip cookies, right? I pushed them toward Robin. "These are for you."

They paused their video. "Why?"

I shrank back at their harsh tone. "'Cause . . . I just . . . thought it'd be nice."

They peered at me through their heavy eyeliner, then took the bag. "Thanks." They started their video again.

"Um, I also wanted to ask if you still hear my music, or if it was just in Spanish."

This time, they pulled down their headphones after pausing the video. "I already told you, if you're worried about people hearing, use headphones."

"I can't. The music doesn't come from my phone." I set my silent phone on the table as proof.

Robin glanced at the phone, and then at me. "So what are you saying?"

"I know this sounds crazy, but—"

"You shouldn't call things crazy."

I blinked. "What?"

"It's dehumanizing to people with mental illness." Their lips pressed together into a thin frown.

"Oh. Sorry. I didn't know." Great. I'd just begun and already I'd said the wrong thing.

"Well, now you do." They took a big stab of their salad.

I slowly spun my phone with my finger. "I just wanted to explain about the fanfare with the test yesterday. You weren't supposed to hear it. Nobody was. It just plays directly in my head and I can't control it."

"What do you mean you can't control it?"

"I just can't. Music's always played wherever I go, fitting whatever I'm doing."

Robin slowly chewed their salad before answering. "Like you're the main character in a movie?"

"Yeah, exactly like that."

"And no one else can hear it?"

"Yeah. You're the first." I rubbed my sweaty palms on my jeans.

"Huh. That explains why Señora Aguilar didn't know what I was talking about." Robin nodded to themself as they grabbed their water bottle and took a swig.

I froze. How long had they been hearing my music? "I'm sorry if it bothered you."

Robin shrugged. "It's a bit distracting, but if there's nothing you can do, there's nothing you can do."

"I guess."

A moment of silence stretched between us. "Well, thanks for letting me know." Robin slipped their headphones back on.

Wait, that couldn't be it. How could they just . . . accept something completely outside the norm? Then again, they were completely outside the norm themself. But wasn't Robin at all curious what it meant? I opened my lunchbag and crunched on some grapes as I considered my options. Be blunt and ask what they thought? No, I didn't want to push them away. Different topic then? Mom did say the best way to make friends was to ask them questions.

"What are you watching?"

They didn't remove their headphones or pause the video. "A telenovela."

"Oh. What's it about?"

Their eyes narrowed. "It's complicated."

"Tell me anyway?"

Robin paused it and turned to me in a huff. "What do you want?"

"I don't know, I just thought . . ."

"What?"

"Don't you want to know why you're the only person who can hear my music?"

"You mean like fate has brought us together, or some crap like that?"

I tried not to wince at the crassness. "I always believed the music was God telling me something. It has to mean something if God allowed you to hear it too."

"I don't believe in God or fate. Just don't bother me, and I won't bother you." They turned back to their telenovela as they took another bite of salad.

That wasn't how this conversation was supposed to go. I numbly picked up my sandwich and shoved it in my mouth. The peanut butter congealed more than usual, drying everything out. *Heavenly Father, what do you want me to do?* "Pink Panther" on the tuba played again in my mind. Yeah, it was a mystery, all right. I sighed and picked up my phone. But instead of searching for memes like usual, I typed 'telenovela' into the search bar.

Latino soap operas, huh? That sounded interesting. I picked one at random that had full episodes available and started to watch.

The entire walk to Spanish the next day, I considered what topics I could have a conversation with Robin about. So, how long have you been playing the tuba? What telenovelas would you recommend? Where did you get all those skulls for your backpack? I squeezed past Señora Aguilar struggling to turn on the projector and settled into my seat. I closed my eyes, said a silent prayer, then turned to Robin. But before I could say anything, they jumped up and started poking at the projector's cords.

After a minute, the screen lit up and the Spirit played a fanfare in my head. Robin jumped at the music and glanced in my direction, but said nothing  as they returned to their seat. I leaned over and whispered, "Buen trabajo," but they just shrugged. I really was just annoying them, wasn't I?

That night, I continued with the telenovela *En Salud*. I understood maybe half of the Spanish, and the subtitles filled me in on the rest. In one of the plotlines, Romina learns she has cancer and decides to break up with her fiance Diego. In response, Diego disguises himself as a chef to deliver food, and as a maid to clean her house, in an effort to win her back. Maybe that's what I need to do to build a relationship with Robin—service.

On Friday night, the band performed at the football game. Allison dropped me off at the school band room before driving to the stadium downtown that we shared with our rival school. I hurried to change into my uniform so I could help Robin carry their instrument to the bus that the band rode together to the game. But when I ran to the back closet, Robin was already settling the wrap-around tuba onto their shoulder. "Hi, want some help?"

Robin's face scrunched up like the lady in the meme trying kombucha for the first time. "Worry about your own instrument."

A sad trombone played. Wah wah waaah. I forced a smile. "Okay. I'll see you on the bus then."

But when it was time to load up, they clomped right past my seat. I banged my head against the window. I was pathetic. I couldn't make a friend even with Heavenly Father's help. Why did being social have to be so hard?

That was it. I gave up.

At the game, I played what I was expected to play and marched what we were supposed to march. But I didn't pay attention to the score. As soon as the band was dismissed, I made a beeline for the bus back to school to get out of the cold. I couldn't wait to crawl into bed and hide under my blanket.

As soon as I sat down in the empty bus, my phone dinged with a text from Allison. *Hey, I'm going to hang out with some people after the game. Is it possible for you to get another ride home?*

A vaguely familiar sad piano melody began to play in my mind, accompanied by violins. Great, now all I needed was for it to start raining. I glared up at the dark clouds that were constant this time of year, but tonight at least, they withheld their drizzle. Mom and Dad were at ward temple night and wouldn't be done for another hour, so I wouldn't be able to ask them for a ride. But who was I to keep Allison from her real friends? I texted back, *Yeah, I can do that.*

Thanks. You're the best! came the reply.

Who else could take me home? Maybe Sister Liang, my Young Women president, could help. I sent her a text, but as the bus slowly filled, there was no reply.

I bit my lip as I tried to think of who else from my Young Women class could drive. Sabrina worked at Subway, but Zoe might be free. I pulled up her number. *Can I ask a favor?*

The seat flumphed as someone dropped down next to me. "Hey, Baylee, are you kay?" Robin asked.

Oh gosh, I didn't look like I was about to cry, did I? I forced a smile. "I'm fine."

"Really? 'Cause you're playing the song from when Romina broke up with Diego in *En Salud.*"

"I am?" I listened more closely to the music. Now that they mentioned it, that did sound right. Under any other circumstances, this would have been a great time to tell them how much I'd enjoyed the telenovela, but I didn't need to see them shut me out again.

Robin nodded. "I could hear it all the way from the stadium entrance."

I glanced back through the window. If they could hear my music from that far away, then they could hear it even if we weren't in the same class. "Oh, my gosh, I am so sorry. I didn't know it had that much range."

"Never mind about that. Did you just get dumped?"

I stared back. "No. I'm not even allowed to date yet."

"Oh." Robin's forehead scrunched up. "Weird that you have a breakup song playing then."

"Yeah." I hoped they would take the hint that I didn't want to talk about it. Otherwise, I might actually cry.

"I know it's not much, but if you had been, I've got some cans in my car I was taking to be recycled. If you need something to smash."

Even if I had been dumped, I imagined I would cope with it with a bucket of ice cream rather than smashing things in a fit of rage. "Thanks, but I'm fine." I forced a bigger smile to prove my point.

"Okay. Night then." Robin clomped down the aisle to a seat two rows back.

As the bus started up to return to school, my phone buzzed with a message from Zoe. *Sorry, I'm babysitting right now.*

I scrolled through my contacts. Who else? "Heavenly Father, please tell me who can give me a ride home," I whispered.

My music faded into silence.

I blinked in disbelief. Nobody? What kind of answer was that? Heavenly Father expected me to wait for my parents, in the cold and dark, alone? But when the bus pulled up next to the school, I had no better answers. So I sent my parents a text and trudged off the bus.

As Robin and the other tuba players passed by with their instruments, I paused. Robin had a car, and their concern had sounded real. Was it okay to ask them for help? They had helped Señora Aguilar without being asked after all.

In answer, Romina and Diego's song started playing again.

I met Robin as they settled their tuba onto the storage rack. "Hey, I think I know why this song is playing."

"Yeah?"

At least they weren't shutting me down this time. "Allison was supposed to give me a ride home, but she ditched me for other friends."

"Well, that's a crappy friend."

"Do you think you could maybe . . . would it be possible for you to give me a ride home? My parents can't get here for another hour." I bit my lip, ready to duck away if they showed annoyance again.

"Where do you live?"

"Over by Griffin Oaks Park."

Robin nodded. "Sure, that's on my way."

"You sure? 'Cause I don't want to bother you if you'd rather not."

Robin shrugged. "I'm not doing anything else tonight. Besides, school's creepy when it's empty. I don't blame you for not wanting to stay."

The tightness in my chest lifted. "Thank you so much. I'll bring you a fresh batch of cookies on Monday."

"You don't have to do that."

"Is there something else you'd prefer? Are you gluten-free?"

"No, it's just that you already got me cookies."

"So? I like making them." I grinned.

Robin smiled slightly. "I suppose if I can't stop you, then I will eat your cookies."

On the drive home, we talked about En Salud and they teased about some upcoming twists. A new tune began to play—a flute and a tuba, melodies chasing each other. Robin laughed. "Could you be more on the nose with that song?"

My cheeks grew suddenly hot. "I'm sorry—"

"What are you sorry for?"

"I dunno. I just. . . I was thinking maybe we should be friends." That was the obvious interpretation. I bit my lip and turned to see Robin's reaction.

"Should be? Like we have to? Like fate?" Their voice sounded harsh, but I caught a glimpse of a smirk.

"I mean, I'd like to be friends." I looked down at my lap. "If you're okay with that."

They glanced at me before shrugging and turning back to the road. "Eh, you don't seem so bad."

I smiled. Well, at least it was a start.

Originally published in Wayfare Magazine (2024).

ANNALIESE (rhymes with pizza) LEMMON likes to eat chocolate, play board games, and collect virtual creatures. Her fiction has been a finalist in the *Mormon Lit Blitz* multiple times, and has appeared in *Mysterion*, *Wayfare*, and *Irreantum*. She lives with her husband and children in Arizona.

Essay

Why Andor's Grown-Up Heroes Matter to Faithful Adults

Alan Hurst

This essay contains spoilers for season one of Andor.

For a Latter-day Saint, I'm unusually interested in alcohol. I've rarely felt tempted to drink it; I know myself well enough to know it wouldn't end well—when the Word of Wisdom speaks to "the weak and the weakest of all saints," I smile and say thankfully, "That's me." And yet the names of unfamiliar spirits can send me down Wikipedia rabbit holes, seeking strange knowledge like the difference between "liquors" and "liqueurs," or ales and lagers, and why James Bond drinks his martinis shaken, not stirred.

It's the culture of the thing that attracts me: the history, the creativity; the vineyards from the Renaissance still run by the same families and the beers hand-brewed by monks; it's the way a beverage (Scotch, bourbon, absinthe) can represent a place or a people or an era; it's all the bottles in all the cellars of the world, filled decades ago by men now dead, waiting to be opened and emptied in an evening.

And we teetotalers get . . . Sprite? No, thanks. I'll just have water.

This essay isn't about alcohol. It's about stories, and specifically about Star Wars' *Andor*, which recently finished its second season on Disney Plus.

In the opening minutes of *Andor*'s first episode, the title character kills two security guards who are trying to rob him. It's all very gritty—ugly weather, dirty cops, nasty red-light district—and on my first uncareful watch, I rolled my eyes. Few pop culture tropes are as tiring as "that show you love, but *dark*."

And then, a bit later, I realized something interesting was going on.

If you haven't watched *Andor*, ask yourself: how would Hollywood usually treat these deaths? The guards were bad guys. They worked for the Empire, if only indirectly, and they were telling the protagonist at gunpoint that he had to give them money or go to jail. If they were in the original Star Wars trilogy, the movie would make sure you forgot them immediately—their dialogue would be limited to "Stop right there!" or "You rebel scum," they'd be wearing helmets to cover their faces, and their voices would be distorted to help you pretend they're not human. For allegedly antifascist art like Star Wars, it's an awfully fascist way to treat people.

In *Andor*, these guys have faces, and their deaths have consequences.

While our protagonist anxiously builds a false alibi, we learn there are detectives on the case—two of them, the inspector and his deputy. The deputy has stayed up all night gathering evidence and thinks he can find the killer in a matter of days, but his boss is about to leave for a performance review where he'll have to report his crime statistics to the Empire. He knows what will happen if he ends his report with, "And by the way, two of my own were bumped off last night."

The inspectors' dialogue deserves an essay of its own. It's an argument between youth and age, zeal and world-wisdom, between an Imperial true believer and a very mild sort of Rebellion—it's even a philosophical contest between deontology and consequentialism—and it's all carried off with a mixture of wit and realism that I can't remember Star Wars ever achieving before. Both inspectors make good points; each is self-serving in ways he won't admit, and if you think it's obvious which decision they should make, then you probably haven't thought the thing through.

And remember, these are the *bad guys*—low-ranking bad guys, no less, invested with agency, intelligence, and humanity. And they're not the only ones.

Ill: Disney+

Prison guards? They have faces, too. We see their sadism, yes, but also their fear of their victims and their frustration with being under-staffed at work.

Imperial soldiers? We see their disappointment with bad assignments and their hope for a better life; we see their heroism, as when an Imperial colonel dies trying to save civilians.

Even in the Empire's Gestapo, we see humanity: a rare woman in the officer corps, determined and talented, her eyes locked on whatever floats beyond the glass ceiling; a senior officer, undoubtedly a wicked war criminal but also a very good boss; a man—just one would-be righteous man—who's realized what he's involved in and desperately wants out.

We've come a long way from "These aren't the droids we're looking for."

There was a golden age of TV recently, or so I've been told. The mostly episodic shows of my childhood were replaced by a new era in which entire multi-season series were planned out before their pilots aired. Successful shows could become something like 40-hour movies, and writers used them to develop characters and themes in ways no visual medium had ever allowed before.

The golden age's brightest gems could usually be found on HBO, whose *The Sopranos* and *The Wire* often appear as numbers 1 and 2 in rankings of the best TV shows of all time, with AMC's *Breaking Bad* also in the conversation. If you follow publications that review pop culture, you could probably name another dozen acclaimed series from the era: *Mad Men*, parts of *Game of Thrones*, *Deadwood*, *Six Feet Under*, *Girls*, *Fleabag*, *The Americans*, and so on.

Yet I've watched very little of this prestige TV for nearly the same reason I've never tried alcohol. I hear the shows have brilliant storytelling, compelling characters, superb production values, real insight into the human condition—and also nudity, violence, persistently obscene language, and often, at their heart, an essentially atheistic and nihilistic philosophy of life.

And we teetotalers get . . . Marvel? Disney? I love *Encanto* and *Coco*, but I get tired of choosing between movies for children and movies for perpetual adolescents. Why is it so hard for a Latter-day Saint grown-up to find a grown-up movie?

I know some of you just rolled your eyes: "Where does this guy get off calling my favorite movies adolescent?" But ask yourself how the typical PG-13 blockbuster presents the world lately, and especially its protagonist. He's usually young and attractive—I say "he," but "strong female characters" often fit the type—and he's defined by two things:

some special gift and some dream or destiny implied by the gift.

The gift and destiny define the story, too: maybe the protagonist knows his destiny, and the story will tell how he and his gift overcame the haters and doubters to attain it, or maybe he doesn't know his destiny, and the story will tell how he discovers it. Either way, the decisive moment comes when the protagonist chooses once and for all to believe in his destiny and believe in himself.

What time of life does that story symbolize if not adolescence, the age of discovering your talents and choosing your career? The story's not about young children, who define themselves by what they love and not yet by gifts and destinies; it's not about the elderly, who have only one grand destiny left and yet often say they're in the happiest time of their lives. It's certainly not about the middle-aged, who are defined less by gifts than by burdens and by the many people who depend on them.

No: today's typical blockbuster, in part for the most practical of box-office reasons, is about the most self-centered decade of American life: 15 to 24, the age when childhood dependency is ending and adult commitments aren't yet formed—when you can choose whatever future you wish, and anything seems possible if you just *want* it hard enough. In fact, it's the age portrayed by the original *Star Wars*, the age of Luke yearning to escape his uncle's farm and "Do or do not; there is no try."

There's nobody like that in *Andor*.

In *Andor*, the rebels' leader is daring and devious, but he can't fight or even know what's going on without his network of guerillas and informers, any one of whom, if caught, could mean the end of him and all his schemes. The rebels' financial backer has plenty of money, but she needs help to cover up what she's doing; the Empire is closing in, and we watch in heartbreaking real time as she discovers she has already sacrificed her family to the cause.

Like human beings, *Andor*'s characters need each other. Like grown-ups, they know it. And so, when they interact—speak, touch, trust, doubt, betray—it actually matters.

Does it make each character less important not to be self-sufficient, not to make a difference by himself—not to have the one gift to rule them all?

Much the opposite. Let me ask you: when was the last time you saw a movie or series whose hero was elderly? I don't mean a show with Harrison Ford or Samuel L. Jackson in his mid-70s, with stunt coordinators straining the limits of their art to pretend he can still beat everyone up. I mean an old person behaving like an old person; in fact,

I mean the true hero of *Andor*, the protagonist's mother, Maarva, a sick old woman hobbling about on a cane.

She hasn't always hobbled. In a flashback, we see her in an adventurous middle age, stealing salvage from a crashed ship minutes before the navy arrives and then risking her life to rescue an orphan from certain death. Later we hear she was the president of some big civic organization. But those days are long past when the show starts, and now she spends most of her time resting in a chair, nagging her aimless son when he's present and fretting while he's away.

Most blockbusters that included such a hero—say, Han Solo in *The Force Awakens*?—would force her through the same adolescent character arc as their protagonist. Her incapacity is all in her mind! She just needs to believe in herself! Then she can prove she's still got it, that she's not so old after all.

Maarva might be the first elderly character I've seen whose heroism doesn't require her to become young again, who conquers with the powers appropriate to old age. It's her experience and wisdom—and even her day-to-day uselessness—that let her see the truth while her younger friends, blinded by daily cares, treat Imperial occupation as just one more of life's hassles to be put up with and outlasted. And when she speaks, it's the love she's earned through a lifetime of service that makes her friends listen.

Not that they want to, not at first; at first, they don't know whether to laugh or cry. What she's taking on is so comically beyond her strength and so likely to cost them her life—forget

> **Someday, our culture won't ask us to choose between childishness and wickedness.**

spies and stormtroopers; if she doesn't stay warm and take her medicine, she's not going to last long enough to be captured. But once again, she sees what they don't: the worth of what's left of her life, and the worth of what she can do with it.

Maarva possesses the power ascribed to Aristotle's unmoved mover: not the power to push or pull or command or control, not the power to move anything by force, but the power to inspire all that know her to move themselves. When the Rebellion finally gets going, it's because they hated the Empire, yes—but it's also because they loved Maarva Andor.

Alcohol won't always be dangerous. I don't know whether its nature will change or ours will, but there will come a day when the saints and their Master drink of the fruit of the vine in His Father's Kingdom, and no alcoholism or drunk driving or domestic violence will follow.

Someday our stories will be safe, too. Someday, "adult" won't mean "pornographic," and "mature" won't mean "nihilistic"; someday, our culture won't ask us to choose between childishness and wickedness.

In the meantime, though, I'll be grateful that healthy grown-up stories aren't *quite* as rare as Word of Wisdom–compliant grown-up drinks, even if, for the moment, our culture shows little interest in either. Star Wars looks set to move on as if *Andor* had never happened, and I expect it to keep spinning out mostly bad, mostly adolescent stories as long as people will still watch them, after which it may well be replaced by something still worse and more adolescent.

But so what? I don't have to watch all that. And if *Andor*'s moral revolution in Star Wars was doomed to fail, at least it had—like Maarva—the wisdom to know it should still try.

Ill: Disney+

Originally published in Public Square Magazine (2025).

ALAN HURST is Latter-day Saint, husband, father, lawyer, and recovering academic.

Fiction

Carta del Cap. Robert Walton a José Smith
por mediación de John Taylor

R. de la Lanza

Loughbrickland, Irlanda
Agosto 2, 1840

Querido Hermano José:

ACATANDO LA PRUDENTE indicación que usted nos dio a los enviados de no dispendiar los recursos como el papel y la tinta en salutaciones y excesivas formalidades, le deseo las bendiciones del Dios Todopoderoso y le comunico que después de sentir el rechazo y la indiferencia de muchos, el Señor ha tocado los corazones de algunos hombres entre quienes escucharon nuestros sermones en Belfast, y ha recibido en Su pueblo a un bendito hombre mediante el bautismo por inmersión, que se llevó a cabo en la tranquilidad del lago Brickland, en un hermoso y pequeño poblado que lleva ese nombre. Se trata del hermano Thomas Tate, de quien daré pormenores en una misiva próxima.

Por ahora me veo compelido a presentar ante usted un asunto peculiar para su consideración especial, dada la singularidad del caso. Justo después de haber oficiado la sagrada ceremonia del bautismo de nuestro ahora hermano Tate, se acercó a mí una joven distinguida por sus modales elegantes y su propiedad para conducirse en sociedad. Me dijo llamarse Maggie Saville, que su tío abuelo había escuchado mi sermón en Belfast y que la había enviado a pedirme que le concediera una plática, aunque sólo fuera por un momento. Su tío abuelo le había encargado hacerme saber que desde hace muchos años lo atormentaban ciertas preguntas muy específicas y que al escuchar mis palabras en ese sermón, supo con certeza que debía buscarme para dar con las respuestas que tanto ha esperado.

Le pregunté a la joven dónde vivía su tío abuelo, dispuesto a acudir en su ayuda, y me dijo que estaba en este mismo lugar, y que me estaba esperando en un mesón, así que fui y subí a sus habitaciones, donde su amable sobrina nos sirvió té y lo procuró, pues aunque se veía un hombre alto y fornido, también se advertía el cansancio de una larga vida llena de trabajos y en su semblante la profundidad de alguien que ha contemplado los rincones más recónditos del alma.

Cuando me vio, el hombre se mostró algo agitado y nervioso. Me habló con una voz grave y ronca, pero no agresiva. Me dijo que su nombre era Robert Walton, y que era un capitán de mar retirado, y que necesitaba con urgencia hallar respuesta a ciertas preguntas que lo atormentaban y le causaban un sufrimiento imposible de describir.

Hermano José: las cosas que este hombre me manifestó haber visto y escuchado sobrepujan la definición de lo que consideramos pecado y los alcances de sentirse extraviado y condenado. Apenas una transgresión que los antiguos griegos llamaban ὕβρις* podría ilustrar la gravedad de las cosas que me relató, si en realidad han ocurrido como él las dice, y me temo que así sea. Por lo tanto, le dije que me consideraba incapaz de presentar sus preguntas del modo adecuado y que sería mucho mejor que él mismo le escribiera a usted, y que, de ser la voluntad de nuestro Dios, usted le respondería.

El hombre entonces hizo una seña a la joven Maggie y ésta sacó de su valija de viaje el paquete de folios manuscritos que le estoy enviando junto a esta carta.

Habiéndome permitido disponer del tiempo y del sagrado llamamiento con que Dios lo ha llamado, le ruego me disculpe y se sirva considerar leer esta misiva para dar respuesta a las interrogantes que atormentan el alma de este pobre hombre, quien, a sus más de ochenta años, dice resistirse a morir sin antes tener la paz en cuanto al asunto.

Suyo en la hermandad del Señor,
    John Taylor,
    élder de la Iglesia de Dios

---

* hybris

Belfast, Irlanda
29 de julio de 1840

Señor profeta José:

Mi nombre es capitán Robert Walton. Mi crianza fue religiosa, como la de la mayoría, pero abandoné la fe cuando conocí la Ciencia y vi cómo se la podía emplear para conseguir cosas hasta ahora inconcebibles, llevarnos a lugares insospechados y librarnos de la esclavitud. Durante mi formación como marinero, además de cumplir con las labores exigentes que el oficio comporta, leí libros de cartografía, astronomía, botánica, y me obsesioné con Aristóteles y sus comentaristas.

Le cuento esto para que valore qué tipo de persona soy y por qué mi ser ha estado turbado desde que encontré a un hombre en la que fue mi última gran expedición. Después de amasar una pequeña fortuna, compré una modesta pero resistente nave, acondicionada para los entornos más helados, contraté hombres de mi confianza y nos hicimos a la mar en el océano Ártico, con la idea de llegar a la cúspide del casco polar, alcanzar el punto exacto del eje de rotación de nuestra noble Tierra, y ver con mis propios ojos si las maravillas y los espantos que se han contado a lo largo de las eras son ciertas o no, como las historias acerca de un lugar paradisiaco en el punto exacto del polo terráqueo o los soleados y verdes parajes de la tierra de la abundancia inagotable.

Yo calculo que no estábamos muy lejos de ese punto, porque la nave comenzó a encallar y a librarse, cada vez con más dificultad. Yo aprovechaba las horas en las que recuperábamos fuerzas para esperar que el casco de nuestra nave, con su peso, rompiera poco a poco los témpanos más delgados y endebles, para escribirle a mi hermana. Pero entonces advertimos lo que inicialmente parecía un animal

Ill: Edward Francis Finden, detail from "Expedition Doubling Cape Barrow, July 26, 1821" (1823), New York Public Library Digital Collections

merodeando nuestra embarcación. Envié hombres a averiguarlo y matar a la criatura con la idea de tener más víveres y de librarnos del peligro, pero al desembarcar, antes de seguir con su pesquisa, vieron a un hombre tirado casi directamente sobre el hielo, expuesto al frío, y a punto del congelamiento.

Lo rescatamos, lo alimentamos y curamos algunas de sus heridas por unos días, hasta que recobró el sentido. Me preguntó quién era yo y qué hacía en esos lugares tan lejanos de la humanidad y la civilización. Tras darle algunos pormenores de mi expedición, y no sin episodios de desmayos, fiebre y dolores, el hombre me relató lo que lo llevaba a él a esos lugares.

Dijo llamarse Víctor, y pertenecer a la aristocracia de Ginebra, específicamente de la rama de los von Frankenstein. En su infancia había presenciado la trágica muerte de su tierna madre a causa de complicaciones en el parto de su hermano menor.

Esa muerte lo hizo perder lo que consideraba una fe firme, y lo hizo ver todo con un rencor y una obsesión inconmensurable por la muerte. De un momento a otro se dio cuenta de que todo tenía el signo de la muerte y de que la vida no es tal, porque su interrupción es inminente. Es caduca porque la muerte es más potente que ella. ¿Cómo puede llamarse vida a un camino en el que todo muere y todos mueren: padres, hermanos, amigos, niños, mujeres, hermanas, esposas... madres... mueren madres y mueren todos en todos los reinos malogrados de la vida?

Y aún con su inevitabilidad, aquel hombre no quiso resignarse a que la muerte estuviera presente en todo. Su obsesión se enquistó cuando recordó el viejo árbol de su casa que, ya seco, retoñó desde sus entrañas después de que lo partiera un rayo en aquella tormentosa noche en que su madre le fue arrebatada. Supo que en ese despliegue de luz había poder, y se decidió a domeñarlo y usarlo para

Ill: Thomas Birch, detail from "Shipwreck near a Rocky Coast" (1833), Art Institute of Chicago.

acabar con la muerte de una vez por todas. Señor profeta José, le suplico no enjuiciar la mentalidad de quienes hemos visto en la Ciencia una diosa voluptuosa que nos ofrece su seno para abrazarnos con su frugalidad. Ni el canto de las sirenas es tan seductor.

El joven Víctor se matriculó entonces en la facultad de medicina de Ingolstadt y se dedicó a aprender como en un frenesí delirante todos los artilugios y las maniobras propias de la medicina moderna, y pronto encontró los principios científicos que podrían sostener teóricamente el modo de evitar la muerte o, por lo menos, de revertirla.

No quiero recordar ni escribirle los horrendos pormenores que el hombre me dio en la cama de mi camarote, que habría de ser el lecho de su muerte, pero lo consiguió: violentamente manipulado por esa frenética ansiedad por acabar con la muerte, llegó a las conclusiones de método adecuadas y puso sus manos a la obra. Pero para que valiera la pena la prueba, debía ser algo notable. No puedo detallarle de dónde y cómo dice este pobre infeliz que se hizo con las partes, elementos y miembros suficientes para confeccionar un cuerpo humano, pero lo hizo, y cuando terminó, tenía un ser semejante a la humanidad, pero nauseabundo y monstruoso. Y no se detuvo. Ahora sabía qué

y cómo hacer para despertarlo de su letargo inanimado.

Los aparatos y máquinas que instaló en su laboratorio bastaron para exponer a ese cuerpo a la fuerza indómita de la naturaleza. Y ocurrió el prodigio: el cuerpo cobró vida. Se movía. Pero luego de unos ligeros movimientos, ocurrieron otros más violentos. Aquel portento ahora vivo se levantó y al hacerlo le causaron al joven galeno un terror tal que se le nubló la mirada y sus manos fueron presa de un frío inclemente. El ser ahora vivo jadeó y rugió, y luego se desplomó en el piso. Nuestro hombre creyó muerta a la criatura y se sintió aliviado, aunque también decepcionado por el fracaso. Pero el horror fue tal que salió corriendo del piso y de la ciudad, y se devolvió a Ginebra, pretendiendo volver a su vida familiar y fingiendo que había perdido el interés por la medicina.

Pero después de un tiempo, la desgracia apareció en su casa, y esta vez no se iba a ir. Víctor se comprometió con su hermana adoptiva, Elisabet, a la que siempre amó, y en el ínterin, acercándose la fecha de la boda, el hermano menor del joven Frankenstein apareció muerto en los jardines de la hacienda. El pequeño se había extraviado y la misma gente que lo buscaba, ahora convertida en una turba multa, culpó a la querida ama de llaves de la casa y la hizo ahorcar en la plaza. Pero Víctor supo que ella no era la responsable. Había sido la criatura. Su criatura, que venía en pos de él y exigía respuestas. Era un auténtico monstruo, un espantoso demonio surgido de la imaginación más atormentada y perversa. Estaba lleno de ira y perpetró destrozos y calamidades para luego exigirle a su creador una entrevista.

El desgraciado aceptó, y en la soledad de la montaña se enfrentó a su creación, quien le dijo que sabía quién era él, y le causó terror al demostrarle que era capaz de hablar, como el más civilizado de los hombres. Llevaba en la mano la que había sido la bitácora de ciencia de Víctor en Ingolstadt, que había olvidado al huir. En esas notas había teorías y reflexiones profanas y antinaturales, pero nunca imaginó que fueran a causar problemas porque para eso haría falta que aquel ser tuviera la capacidad de leer.

Y, asístanos la cordura, la criatura sabía leer y lo hacía muy bien. No había escape. El pobre médico preguntó al portento qué quería. Éste le mostró la libreta y le dijo: "Busco respuestas". La criatura sabía leer, señor Profeta del Señor. No me pregunte cómo, que se me parte el alma de recordarlo, pero básteme decirle que el monstruo sabía leer.

Le preguntó a Victor si era su padre, dado que lo había creado, o si sólo era el producto de un capricho con el cual se había divertido. Y si era su padre, la pregunta era si tenía amor por él, por su hijo. Preguntó si tenía un nombre. Si, como buen padre, lo conocía, o por lo menos sabía quiénes eran las personas cuyas partes mutiladas integraban su cuerpo, si su inteligencia era suya o del dueño de la parte involucrada con ella. Y preguntó quién era él ante Víctor, si su existencia tenía un propósito, y cuál era ese propósito.

Luego la criatura le dijo que en su peregrinar había aprendido sobre el alma, y preguntó: "¿Tengo un alma, padre? ¿Me diste un alma?"

"¿Tengo un alma, padre? ¿Me diste un alma?"

Apreciable señor Profeta: su enviado, el de la voz sabia, habla de que a través de usted Dios da respuestas, por favor, le suplico que me ayude a saber qué podía haber respondido este hombre desgraciado al deforme ser al que había dado vida y que demandaba palabras de sabiduría y consuelo.

Algunas noches después de que el dr. Víctor von F. Me contara su desgraciada vida, se sintió con fuerzas para levantarse y arengar a mis hombres, quienes ya estaban en vías de amotinarse. Y tras una reunión en la que pude calmar a toda la tripulación con el anuncio de que volvíamos a casa sin alcanzar nuestra meta, volví al camarote para ver cómo seguía nuestro huésped y vi a la criatura de pie junto al cuerpo inerte y sin vida de su autor. La criatura lloraba y con una facilidad inusitada levantó a Victor y se lo llevó.

Para todos la pesadilla había terminado, pero para mí comenzó. Señor profeta, su enviado ha hablado de lo que él llama el plan de Dios para con todos los hombres, y de un milagroso poder que ha de revertir para siempre la muerte. Yo no deseo tanto. Sólo quiero dormir en paz. Y por eso confío en que usted, con su bendito don y la inteligencia natural que asiste a todos los hombres, entienda todas las otras preguntas que entraña mi deplorable situación. Debo saber responder a las preguntas de aquel engendro, pues no sé si algún día lo volveré a ver o si me sorprenderá en mis sueños, y necesito responderle o, por lo menos, saber para mí mismo esas respuestas.

Le envío mi gratitud y parabienes.
Cptn. Robert Walton

R. DE LA LANZA (Ciudad de México, 1977) es escritor, editor literario y músico. Ha sido periodista cultural y enseña escritura literaria. Es autor de Eleusis, una novela que cuenta la historia de cuatro generaciones de miembros de La Iglesia de Jesucristo de los Santos de los Últimos Días en México.

Fiction

A Letter from Captain Robert Walton to Joseph Smith, *Care of John Taylor*

R. de la Lanza

translated by
Ryan Fairchild and DA Cooper

Loughbrickland, Ireland
August 2, 1840

Dear Brother Joseph,

Following your wise instruction to us messengers not to waste resources like paper and ink on greetings and excessive formalities, I wish you the blessings of Almighty God and inform you that, after experiencing the rejection and indifference of many, the Lord has touched the hearts of some men among those who heard our sermons in Belfast and has received into His people a blessed man through baptism by immersion, which took place in the tranquility of Brickland Lake, in a beautiful little village of that name.

That man is Brother Thomas Tate, about whom I will give details in a forthcoming letter.

For now, I feel compelled to present a peculiar matter for your special consideration, given the strangeness of the case. Just after I had officiated at the sacred ceremony of the baptism of our now Brother Tate, a young woman approached me, distinguished by her elegant manners and propriety. She told me her name was Maggie Saville, that her great-uncle had heard my sermon in Belfast and had sent her to ask me to grant him a conversation, even if only for a moment. Her great-uncle had charged her with informing me that for many years he had been tormented by certain very specific questions and that upon hearing my words in that sermon he knew with certainty that he should seek me out to find the answers he had so long awaited.

I asked the young woman where her great-uncle lived, ready to attend to his need, and she told me that he was in this very town, awaiting me in an inn. And so I went to the inn and up to his room where his kind niece served us tea and looked after him, for although he was a tall and strong man, one could also see the weariness of a long life full of labor, and in his countenance the depth of one who has contemplated the hiddenmost corners of the soul.

When he saw me, the man seemed somewhat agitated and nervous. He spoke to me in a deep, hoarse voice, but not aggressively. He told me his name was Robert Walton, that he was a retired sea captain, and that he urgently needed to find answers to certain questions that tormented him and caused him indescribable suffering.

Brother Joseph, the things this man told me he saw and heard surpass all understanding of what we consider sin and the limits of what it means to be godforsaken and condemned. Only a transgression that the ancient Greeks called ὕβρις* could capture the gravity of the things he related to me, if they really happened as he says, and I fear that they did. Therefore, I told him that I felt incapable of posing his questions properly and that it would be much better if he wrote to you himself, and that, God willing, you would answer him.

The man then signaled to young Maggie, and she took out of her travel bag the packet of handwritten pages that I am sending you along with this letter.

Having been granted the time and the sacred calling with which God has called me, I beg you to excuse me and please consider reading this letter to answer the questions that

---

* hubris

Ill: Edward Francis Finden, detail from "Expedition Doubling Cape Barrow, July 26, 1821" (1823), New York Public Library Digital Collections

torment the soul of this poor man, who, at over eighty years of age, says he refuses to die without first having peace regarding the matter.

Yours in the brotherhood of the Lord,
John Taylor,
Elder of the Church of God

Belfast, Ireland
July 29, 1840

To the Honorable Prophet Joseph Smith:

My name is Captain Robert Walton. My upbringing was religious, like most, but I abandoned the faith when I discovered Science and saw how it could be used to achieve things previously inconceivable, take us to unimaginable places, and free us from bondage. During my training as a sailor, in addition to fulfilling the demanding duties of the profession, I read books on cartography, astronomy, and botany, and I became obsessed with Aristotle and his commentators.

I tell you this so that you may appreciate what kind of person I am and why my very being has been haunted since I met the man on what was my last great expedition. After amassing a small fortune, I bought a modest but sturdy ship, equipped for the coldest environments, hired men I trusted, and set sail in the Arctic Ocean with the idea of reaching the summit of the polar ice cap, reaching the exact point of the Earth's axis of rotation, seeing with my own eyes whether the wonders and horrors that have been recounted throughout the ages are true or not, such as the stories about a paradisiacal place at the exact point of the Earth's pole or the sunny and green landscapes of the land of inexhaustible abundance.

I estimate that we were not far from that point because the ship began to run aground and only with increasing difficulty could we free her. I used the hours when we were recovering our strength, waiting for the hull of our ship with its weight to gradually break through the thinnest and most fragile ice floes, to write to my sister. But then we noticed what initially appeared to be an animal prowling around our vessel. I sent men to investigate and kill the creature, hoping to have more provisions and be rid of the danger, but upon disembarking and before continuing their search, they saw a man lying on the ice, exposed to the cold, already on the verge of freezing.

We rescued him, fed him, and treated his wounds for a few days until he regained consciousness. He asked me who I was and what I was doing so far removed from humanity and civilization. After giving him some details of my expedition, and not without episodes of fainting, fever, and pain, the man told me what had brought him to that place.

He said his name was Victor and that he belonged to the Geneva aristocracy, specifically the von Frankenstein branch. In his childhood, he had witnessed the tragic death of his young mother due to complications during the birth of his younger brother. That death caused him to lose what he considered a firm faith and made him see everything with an immeasurable resentment and an obsession with death. From one moment to the next, he realized that everything bore the mark of death and that life is not life at all because its interruption is imminent. It is ephemeral because death is more powerful than life. How can such a path be called life, a path where everything and everyone dies—parents, siblings, friends, children, women, sisters, wives . . . mothers . . . where even mothers die, where everyone dies in every ill-fated realm of life?

And yet, despite its inevitability, that man refused to accept that death was ever-present. His obsession deepened when he remembered the old tree in his yard, which, though withered, sprouted new growth from its roots after being struck by lightning on that stormy night when his mother was taken from him. He knew that in that display of light there was power, and he resolved to tame it and use it to end

death once and for all. Mr. Smith, I beg you not to judge the mindset of those of us who have seen in Science a voluptuous goddess offering us her bosom to embrace us with her economy. Not even the song of the sirens is so seductive.

The young Victor then enrolled in the medical faculty of Ingolstadt and devoted himself to learning, as if in a delirious frenzy, about all the devices and maneuvers of modern medicine, and soon found the scientific principles that could theoretically support the way to avoid death or, at least, to reverse it.

I do not want to recall or write down the horrifying details the man gave me from my cabin bed, which was to be his deathbed, but he succeeded; violently driven by that frenzied anxiety to end death, he came to sufficient methodological conclusions to begin his labors. But for the trial of his theory to be worthwhile, it had to be something remarkable. I cannot tell you where and how this poor wretch claims to have obtained enough parts, elements, and limbs to construct a human body, but he did, and when he finished he had a being resembling humanity, but nauseating and monstrous. And he did not stop there. Now he knew how to awaken it from its inanimate slumber.

The apparatus and machines he installed in his laboratory were enough to expose that body to the untamed force of nature. And the miracle occurred: the body came to life. It moved. But after a few slight movements, more violent ones followed. That now-living marvel rose up, and as it did so, it caused the young doctor such terror that his vision blurred and his hands were gripped by an unforgiving cold. The now-living being gasped and roared and then collapsed to the floor. Our man believed the creature dead and felt relieved, though also disappointed by the failure. But the horror was such that he ran out of the apartment and the city and returned to Geneva, pretending to go back to his family life and feigning that he had lost interest in medicine.

But after a while, misfortune struck at home and would not leave. Victor became engaged to his adopted sister, Elisabeth, whom he had always loved. But as the wedding date drew near, his younger brother was found dead in the gardens of the estate. The little boy had gone missing, and the same people who had been searching for him, now a mob, blamed the family's beloved housekeeper and had her hanged in the town square. But Victor knew she was not responsible. It was the creature. His creature who was coming after him and demanding answers. It was a true monster, a hideous demon born from the most tormented and perverse imagination.

The monster was filled with anger and perpetrated destruction and calamities only to then demand an interview with his creator.

The unfortunate man accepted, and in the solitude of the mountain he confronted his creation, who told Victor that he knew who he was and terrified Victor by demonstrating that he was capable of speech, like the most civilized of men. In his hand he carried what had been Victor's science logbook from Ingolstadt, which he had forgotten when he fled. In those notes were profane and unnatural theories and reflections, but he never imagined they would cause such chaos. For that to occur, this being would have needed to have the ability to read.

And, may sanity prevail, the creature knew how to read, indeed very well. There was no escape. The poor doctor asked the marvel what it wanted. It showed him the notebook and said, "I seek answers." The creature knew how to read, Mr. Smith. Do not ask me how, for it breaks my heart to recall, but suffice it to say that the monster knew how to read.

He asked if Victor was his father since he had created him, or if he was merely the product of a whim Victor had indulged in. And if he was his father, the question was whether he loved him, his son. He asked if he had a name. If, like any good father, he knew him, or at least knew who the people were whose mutilated parts made up his body, if his intelligence was his own or that of the owner of the part involved with it. And he asked who he was in Victor's eyes, if his existence had a purpose, and what that purpose was.

Then the creature told him that in his wanderings he had learned about the soul, and asked: "Do I have a soul, Father? Did you give me a soul?"

Dear Mr. Smith, your messenger, the one with the wise voice, speaks of how God gives answers through you. Please, I beg you to help me understand what this unfortunate man could have answered to the deformed being he had brought into being, who demanded words of wisdom and comfort.

A few nights after Dr. Victor von F. had told me about his unfortunate life, he felt strong enough to rise and harangue my men, who were already on the verge of mutiny. And after a meeting in which I was able to calm the entire crew by announcing that we were returning home without achieving our goal, I went back to the cabin to see how our guest was doing and saw the creature standing beside the inert, lifeless body of his creator. The creature was weeping and with unusual ease lifted Victor and carried him away.

For everyone else, the nightmare was over, but for me, it was just beginning. Mr. Smith, your messenger

"Do I have a soul, Father? Did you give me a soul?"

has spoken of what he calls God's plan for all mankind and of a miraculous power that will forever reverse death. I do not desire so much. I only want to sleep in peace. And so I trust that you, with your blessed gift and the natural intelligence that all men possess, will understand all the other questions that my deplorable situation entails. I must know how to answer the questions of that creature, for I do not know if I will ever see him again or if he will surprise me in my dreams, and I need to answer him or, at least, know those answers for myself.

I send my gratitude and best wishes.
Captain Robert Walton

R. DE LA LANZA was born and lives in Mexico City. He is a writer, writing coach and musician. He has experience in culture journalism and teaches literary writing. He is the author of *Eleusis: The Long and Winding Road*, a novel that tells the story of four generations of Latter-day Saints in Mexico.

Poetry

FROM A SPIRIT TO THE ONE POSSESSED

ORSON SCOTT CARD

I know you conjured me, but not from hell;
I came in light, but I was not aflame.
You should be careful of the powers you name,
For some are deaf, while others hear too well.

When you were through with me, you bade me leave;
You gathered up and put away my bones;
You cast a broken spirit on the stones,
Never thinking that I might deceive.

Are you having trouble with your heart?
Does it flutter when you stand too long?
Is there something crawling in your womb?
At last you've come to doubt your failing art,
And frail with terror is your fending song;
Ah, lovely one: Your body is my home.

Originally published in An Open Book *(2004).*

ORSON SCOTT CARD is the author of the novels *Ender's Game, Ender's Shadow,* and *Speaker for the Dead.* His most recent series are the young adult Pathfinder series, the fantasy Mithermages series, and the Side Step series. Besides these and other science fiction novels, Card has written contemporary fantasy, biblical novels, the American frontier fantasy series *The Tales of Alvin Maker,* poetry, and many plays and scripts. He currently lives in Greensboro, North Carolina, with his wife, Kristine Allen Card.

VOICES FROM THE DUST

JEANNA MASON STAY

It's not like I was *trying* to turn Samantha's bedroom into a storage closet. But when she left for BYU in August . . . well, it just happened. It started with little things, like when I accidentally ordered ten cases of green chiles instead of ten cans. The pantry was full, the area under our bed packed with dried beans and canned white wheat. So I shoved the cases in her closet.

Next was a pile of books I bought for Jacob's birthday. I hid them under her desk. An extra supply of toilet paper went on her bed, an emergency chocolate stash behind her chair. I could easily clear it all out by the time she came home for summer break.

But then my grandmother died, and I inherited fifteen giant tubs of craft supplies. Whoever said collecting craft supplies and actually crafting were two separate hobbies had obviously met Oma.

So I stashed them in Samantha's room and promised myself I'd

sort through them long before the beginning of May.

Fast forward.

To March.

To a little countdown calendar sitting on our kitchen table reminding us it was only "five more weeks till Samantha comes home!"

I stood in the doorway, staring in horror at the wall of bins before me. What had Oma always said? The only way out was through? Okay, through I'd go. I opened the first bin and sneezed. Apparently her craft supplies hadn't been used anytime this century.

And then I heard a voice.

It was like the Holy Ghost, except this voice was Oma's. And she was telling me to write a limerick.

I ignored it. The Holy Ghost had never sounded like Oma before, so this was clearly just some weird form of grieving. I pulled out a baggie full of colored pencils.

I heard the voice again: "*Ginny-girl, don't you ignore me.*" That was Oma's nickname for me, the one she used when she was about to lecture.

Even now, it made me squirm.

I sighed. I knew it was ridiculous, but it couldn't hurt. Right? So I pulled a marker from the bin and started thinking. *T-rex . . . Lex . . . something about bricks?* Shakespeare I am not.

When I finished writing the pathetic thing, it needed embellishing, obviously. I rewrote the poem with flourishes and multiple marker colors. The bin also had a pile of stickers, so I hunted for a dinosaur sheet and added a few purple dinos.

"*Now put it in your purse.*"

I rolled my eyes. Sure, Oma. But I'd already humored the absurdity of the first instruction, so I might as well keep going. I was about to return to actually cleaning when my alarm went off. Time to pick Lucas up from school.

At pickup, I noticed a little girl sitting alone, looking glum. My purse, and the limerick, suddenly felt heavy on my shoulder. Why not? I sat beside her. "Do you like dinosaurs?"

Fifteen minutes later, Lucas had a new friend and I had the undying gratitude of a t-rex enthusiast holding a very bad limerick in her sweaty palms.

Weird. But the Spirit does work in mysterious ways, apparently even through Oma.

The next day, digging through her cake-making supplies, I found a unicorn mold. *"Make a zebra unicorn cake."* I looked at the clock and then at my to-do list. I didn't have time for this. *"Make the darned cake, Ginny-girl."*

Fine. I made the cake. When my next-door neighbor came by to vent about how she'd forgotten her daughter's highly specific birthday cake request, I was ready.

Next it was fabric markers. *"Drive them to the church. Now."* So I did, and Sister Miyaki stood outside, surrounded by a gaggle of activity day kids holding white t-shirts. She looked about to cry.

"Sister Johnson will be here with the tie dye supplies any minute," she said with a smile, obviously fake. Then she spotted me. "Oh, Sister Alberry! What brings you here?"

I handed her the box with a hug. "Will these help?" I whispered.

Relief swept across her face. "Change of plans!" She clapped. "We're going to draw our favorite scripture stories on the t-shirts."

I smiled and left. I still had a lot of cleaning to do.

"Take the cotton batting and leave it on Brother Langley's front porch. Don't ring the doorbell." So I loaded up three garbage sacks and drove them over to leave at his door. I never learned what came of that one, but Brother Langley did have a toddler with a terrible sense of balance.

Next it was *"crochet an octopus."* I hadn't crocheted since Lucas was a baby, but I hauled out the softest pink yarn from one of the bins and went to work. The next day was an ocean-themed baby shower I'd forgotten for a new mom in our ward.

Papier mâché, small quilting projects, donations to local hospitals and senior centers, a misshapen little dragon made entirely of shells. I wasn't getting a lot of actual cleaning done, but the craft supplies were still dwindling.

Somehow, before I knew it, I'd flown through almost all of the bins. Where had all those supplies gone? It felt a little like the miracle of the fishes and loaves, except in reverse—surely I couldn't have run out of everything so quickly?

Still, it was nearly the end of April, and I was finally down to the last bin.

I opened it and waited for yet another ridiculous demand. But there was only silence. The box was full of paper and markers, much fancier than what I'd used for my shaky, poorly written limerick. I riffled the creamy paper, remembering how I'd loved the feeling of the marker in my hand.

I hadn't spent much time crafting in the last decade—life had gotten busy, and I had no regrets about that. But Oma's craft supplies had been like warm sunshine and soft rain, and suddenly I wanted to grow and expand and try new things like I hadn't for years. I loved making beautiful things. It was good to remember.

I pulled out a piece of paper—the thick, luxurious kind I would normally have reserved for "something special." Which meant I would never use it at all. I stared at it for a moment, then began to draw. The fire-breathing giraffe dragon I ended up with half an hour later wouldn't be winning any awards any time soon, but Lucas would love it. I smiled as I went to set it on his pillow for him to find after school.

I guess I didn't need Oma's voice to tell me what to do anymore.

I dragged the bin of markers and paper out of Samantha's room and into my own closet for safe keeping. This box I would keep.

I brushed my hands together and closed Samantha's bedroom door with a satisfied sigh. Time to tackle the pantry I'd been avoiding. I grabbed a rag and began with the top shelf, swiping a rag across the layer of dust adorning a row of #10 cans of quick oats. No one would ever accuse me of being a spotless homemaker.

The voice of my old ministering sister spoke in my head: *"Make a gallon of oatmeal."*

I closed my eyes for a minute, took a deep breath, then went to find a pot.

JEANNA MASON STAY mostly writes and edits fantasy and romance, but she also loves creating intimate peeks into loving but imperfect families and exploring how the gospel and the scriptures affect how we see the world. She misses Alice Springs, Australia, where she lived with her handsome husband, four charming children, and zero pets (if you don't count all the rocks). But Utah is nice too. Jeanna loves fireflies, serial commas, birds of paradise, and galahs. She dreams of one day owning a herd of Chia sheep. Find her on Instagram @jeannamasonstay and at jeannamasonstay.com.

First Light:
Early LDS Speculative Writing

GRANDMOTHER'S ROCKING CHAIR

NEPHI ANDERSON

with introduction by Kent Larsen

While Nephi Anderson's "Grandmother's Rocking Chair" can be categorized as speculative fiction, it is also an attempt to use Mormon history to influence young church members to remain faithful to the church. Published in The Contributor *in May 1890, just a few months following his first story's publication, "Grandmother's Rocking Chair" appeared early in the Home Literature movement, and just a year after Anderson's popular* A Young Folk's History of the Church *appeared.*

Similar to Mark Twain's A Connecticut Yankee in King Arthur's Court, *published just a few months before, "Grandmother's Rocking Chair" suggests that the main character travels to the past by way of accident. While the timing is tight for Anderson to have been inspired by Twain's novel, it also followed Edward Bellamy's* Looking Backward (1888) *and William Morris's* A Dream of John Ball (*published serially*

in 1886 and as a book in 1888), both of which use similarly vague devices for sending a character to another point in time.

Despite the relatively short time since the publication of Anderson's first story, "Grandmother's Rocking Chair" shows improvement in Anderson's writing. Ben, who seems to be somewhere between 10 and 16 years old, is acting rudely under the influence of friends. When his family is gone one night, he sits in his grandmother's rocking chair and travels to November 1838, where he experiences the persecutions of the Mormon expulsion from Missouri. But before he suffers bodily harm, he is miraculously returned to his own time.

The evocative personalization of the historical events of the Missouri War overwhelm the concerns of Ben's present life—perhaps undermining the plausibility of his initial grumpiness. And in the end, the story's claim that Ben will feel grateful following his experience in 1838 Missouri doesn't quite seem plausible, since it suggests that his gratitude comes from feeling the suffering of those who lived 50 years earlier.

- Kent Larsen

WHAT TO BE SO THANKFUL for, I can't see."

"Benjamin South, what ails you to-night? I have never seen you in such grumbling spirits before."

"Well, I have never had so much cause to grumble, as you call it, before, I guess. That's the reason. You are continually talking of being thankful, about what I don't understand. If ever person had cause to complain, I have."

"Why, Ben South, I'm astonished at you! Haven't you enough to eat, good clothing to wear, a comfortable home, a good position, surrounded by the best of society and—well, I'm perfectly amazed—" and a pair of bright, blue eyes stared straight at the object of her wonder, and the exclamation came to a sudden stop as if in utter bewilderment.

Back in the corner of the room Grandma South sat listening to the animated discussion. She had even dropped her knitting on her lap, and sat looking at the disputants. Grandma was thoroughly aroused sure, as it took more than an ordinary occurrence to stop the click, click, of her needles.

"Well, now, don't let it take your breath away, Sis; you'll need it to enumerate all those blessings I enjoy." Ben's sarcastic tone had its effect on his sister. It pained her sensitive nature and grandma saw it and came to the rescue.

Ben greatly respected his grandmother. The wrinkled features crowned with snow-white locks combed back smoothly over her forehead, presented a beautiful and sacred appearance. No matter how much trouble Ben caused his mother and sister, when grandma spoke, he was conquered.

Grandma motioned Ben to sit down by her side, which he did, trying to smooth things over with a good-natured laugh.

"So my boy has nothing to be thankful for?" she said.

"Why, grandma, thanks giving is a long way off yet."

"Is it? I thought it was with us always. Now I want you to tell me your troubles," and she laid her hand gently on his arm. "Give me an account of your trials and sufferings that are afflicting you so, and I will try to secure a remedy."

Appealed to thus directly, Ben was thrown into confusion, and he felt that his stumbling excuses were very poor explanations of what he had so grumbled about. Now the truth of the matter was that Ben had no more cause for discontent than the majority of Utah's boys have. As his sister had said, he lacked for none of the necessaries of life, and enjoyed many of its comforts. The reason for this unsatisfied condition of his mind Ben hardly knew himself, and in the only place where it could be found, he failed to look, namely—within himself. True to human nature, that

was the last place he would search. It was simply a case of neglected duty and the accompanying results—a loss of the Spirit of God. Ben had formed the acquaintance of some of the boys of the city who were not of the class that attend Sabbath schools and Mutual Improvement

Now the truth of the matter was that Ben had no more cause for discontent than the majority of Utah's boys have.

Associations. These companions had led him from his duty and enticed him into many of their ways, and Ben was in danger of becoming as wild and reckless as they. Mingling with these evil influences Ben's mind became dark at times, and a feeling of doubt would often creep into his reasonings as to the truth of his religion. Of course this was only on occasions. He had not yet expressed himself in this way, but at the rate he was going, it would not take long to reach that point.

Grandma South was in the habit of talking to Ben on the principles of the Gospel; and as he sat by her side this evening she enumerated the blessings that he enjoyed, the greatest of all being the privilege of having the Gospel of Christ in its fullness and purity, and having access to its many blessings. She told him that in her youth this was one of the few advantages that she had enjoyed unmolested; which subject branched, as it usually did, to her early days, spent among the persecutions of Missouri and Illinois. Ben generally listened with a great deal of pleasure to these narratives of his grandmother's, but this evening he found himself comparing her simple

Grandma's rocking chair was a coveted piece of furniture, and in consequence was seldom unoccupied.

accounts with far different ones he had heard from his companions, and read about in books loaned him by them, which pictured the early events of the Church in very dissimilar colors. Poor fellow, he was not wise enough to decide between them, and so his mind became darker and the scene of greater confusion than ever.

"Come, Ben, are you not going to the party to-night? It is getting late," called his mother from the doorway of the kitchen.

"No!" answered Ben abruptly.

Sister South (Widow South she was sometimes called, as she had been a widow for a number of years) was a little startled by her son's answer; not so much by the tone, for, sorry to say, it was often harsh lately, as by the fact that he was not going to the dance, as he seldom missed a ward party.

Gertie's escort now arrived, and soon departed with a partner. Brother Olsen and his wife called soon after and persuaded Sister South to accompany them to the party. Grandma gathered up her stockings and ball of yarn withdrawing to her own room and to bed.

The house became still, and Ben was left alone. He went to the hearth, and adding more fuel to the fire, drew grandma's rocking chair up to the blaze, and seated himself comfortably. Now, grandma's rocking chair was a coveted piece of furniture, and in consequence was seldom unoccupied. If you could have sat in it once, you would soon have found the secret of this. In the seat was the cushion which mother had stuffed with the best duck feathers, and Gertie had adorned with fancy work in the shape of borders and flowers. The high back covered with a neat tidy, made such an easy rest for a tired head. Then you could rock as gently or as vigorously as you pleased and feel perfectly safe. That chair was made to last; that was shown by its stout hickory frame and raw-hide seat and back. Oh, it was a wonderful household article! It had even crossed the plains, strapped on behind the ox cart; so it was a sacred heir-loom in the family.

The fire in the grate blazed up cheerfully and cast a rudy light throughout the room. Ben leaned back in his chair and watched the flames in their wild frolic. How they danced and leaped! now quivering near the glowing coals, and now leaping up into fantastic shapes. Now a fiery arm would reach out as if to grasp some unseen foe, and then playfully jerk it back again. Then it would strive to ascend the great, black chimney's throat; up and down, back and forth, round and round went the capricious flames till they made Ben's head fairly swim to look at them. Even grandmother's rocking chair began to be disturbed. As Ben watched he saw the fire stretch out a flaming arm, and the chair, nothing loath, joined its arm with it, and they actually danced! That old, sensible, stay-at-home chair with its glowing partner waltzed and polkaed, and wheeled and spun round and round. Well, Ben hung on for dear life, frightened nearly out of his wits. At the same time he felt like laughing outright at the strange spectacle. He surely would, had it not been for the feeling that everything was scarcely right in this wild whirl.

At last they stopped, and Ben breathed easier. The old chair had stood the ordeal well. In fact it seemed to have gathered a newness of life in its dizzy flight. As Ben examined it, it certainly did look like a new chair, just out of the workshop. In the excitement the cushion and tidy had disappeared, and all the little draperies and ornaments had been shaken off. But now his attention was drawn to something else. The room itself had undergone a change; it had become smaller; the walls had become rougher as if made of logs; the pictures on the walls had diminished wonderfully in both quantity and quality; everything was as neat and scrupulously clean as ever, but Oh, how bare and cheerless it had become!

In wonder Ben stepped to the door and looked out. It was broad day. An autumn haze hung over the earth. The mountain which greeted him every morning was not there. On his right as far as the eye could reach stretched the rolling prairie. On the left was a dense forest about three miles wide, following the course of a river. Farmhouses dotted the landscape, most of which showed signs of having been recently erected;

still they had an air of comfort and thrift about them. Much of the prairie had been brought under cultivation, and had been converted into fruitful fields and gardens. The ring of distant choppers came from the wood; the plowman had left his furrow, and the herd-boy was putting up the bars of the corral.

On the sunny side of the house Ben encountered two children, a boy and a girl. They were playing. Wrapped up in their innocent sport, they were enjoying themselves as only children can, as only age can appreciate. The little girl was dressed in a plain garment made of some home-made material. Woolen stockings and a pair of well worn shoes decked the pattering feet. A blue gingham sunbonnet lay on the grass. A pair of bright blue eyes looked out from under the fine, light-colored hair which the breeze tossed about her forehead. Not many summers she had seen, yet each had left a rosy kiss on her cheeks. The boy, her brother, had on an old straw hat set well back on his head. His unruly locks had stolen out through a rent in the crown and were waving majestically in the air. One suspender held up the pantaloons, a re-make of his father's, and the bare, brown feet scorned the idea of being imprisoned in shoes.

A number of birds were flying overhead; they seemed to have found a comfortable retreat in the gable of the roof where the cornice should have been. The children were busy making a nest of mud as they had seen the swallows do in the spring. After a failure or two, they succeeded in making one stick to the log. As they stepped back to admire their work, the litttle girl said to her brother, "I think the birds might come and live in it. It will take them such a long time to build one, they're so little you know." At this they both retreated to give them a chance, but as no notice was taken of this proffered residence by the birds, the children, determining to have somebody live in it, set out chasing a gay butterfly that was lazily flitting by.

Someone motioned to Ben from the doorway; answering the summons, he saw a woman that he had seen before, but where or when he could not call to mind.

"Well, Benjamin, I see you've come. I'm glad of it. I am in need of someone like you just now—oh, don't stare so—my name is Grandma South. Of course you don't understand that now, but you will soon enough. Now won't you go to the clearing and get some wood? then we shall have some supper."

Ben started to do as he was asked. It was all a little strange at first, but he soon took it all without much surprise, and ere long it came natural enough; and so he thought no more about it.

Ben was about to return with his load, when he heard a swift, sharp clatter of horses' hoofs coming down the road. The children stopped playing. They stood still and listened, and as a body of armed men came in sight, all signs of childish joy vanished from their little faces, and a look of terror came into their eyes. With frantic haste they turned and sped towards home, crying as they fled—"The mob, they're coming, they're coming, O, mother, mother!"

A band of men—mobbers, for such they proved to be—came upon them with a dash. The mother, trying to soothe her terrified children, stood still upon the doorstep awaiting their coming. The mob wheeled their horses round the house, while with brandished weapons the leader rode to the door and enquired whether her husband was at home.

The little woman, pale though she were and struggling hard to appear calm, with her children clinging to her, faced them with look and attitude of unflinching courage. Not a word she spoke, but met their fiendish looks with a steady eye. The leader leaped from his horse and throwing his bridle to another, bade some others follow him. With a brutal push the mother was sent from the doorstep, while the children screamed with terror. With horrible oaths they swore vengeance on the husband should they find him, and entering the house, began tumbling the furniture about in their endeavors to secure the object of their search. Finding their efforts in vain, in their rage they overturned and destroyed the few simple articles of comfort

Ill: CCA Christensen, detail from "Saints Driven from Jackson County Missouri" (1878), Brigham Young University Museum of Art.

and ornament which the wife had arranged by her diligence and toil. As they mounted again, the leader, swinging his saber in the air, exclaimed with an oath, "We'll be back in thirty minutes. If you're not out of this by then, the roof might hurt you as it tumbles in!" With this they galloped across the fields to a neighbor's.

"Well," asked Ben, who had just come up, "What does this mean?"

"It means," was the reply, "that the mob are doing what they have threatened to do all summer."

"And what is that?"

"Drive us from the county. We had placed some reliance in the Governor's promised protection, but it seems to have been in vain and we are doomed. Great heavens! see! The mobbers are coming back! They suppose you to be my husband. Come, help me with the children. They will do as they have said!" But ere they could each lift a child and gain the woods, the mobbers were again upon them. A crowd of wild, maddened beings they were; as they overtook and surrounded the fugitives, they saw their mistake in supposing they had captured the object of their wrath. "They are making tracks," shouted one, "let them go. We'll see that they don't come back again!" with which they rode up to the log dwelling, which was home at least to the women and children, and proceeded to

demolish the roof. As the fugitives looked back they saw it cave in and become a shapeless ruin.

A cold, dismal, November evening came on. The sky was being hidden by clouds, and the chilly winds blew with a bitter keenness. No time had been given the exiles in which to prepare, or wrap themselves in extra clothing, and soon the children's teeth began to chatter with cold; so they were set down to run awhile. Soon on their right they saw a sheet of flame appearing above the treetops. "They are setting fire to the houses! See, that must be Brother L---'s place! And there is another!" the mother exclaimed as another and still another column of blaze pierced the heavens and lighted up the woods and prairies.

When the little party had traveled far enough to be out of immediate danger, a rest was taken. And now as the full force of what had befallen them broke upon the mother, she could not contain herself longer. Her husband was expected home that evening. He had only gone to Independence that morning; if he should escape the mobs and return home—home did she say—a ruin, perhaps a heap of ashes! No wife, no children—and the heartbroken wife burst out in a fit of weeping! Ben did all in his power to help. He suggested that they try to find a neighbor's, but was reminded of the fact that they had none, all had been driven out like themselves. Ben could think of nothing else. He was powerless to materially aid. But the mother's burst of grief soon subsided; she had her children to think of, to care for, and it would not do to give up.

For hours they wandered aimlessly about the woods. Now and then could still be seen the red glare of some burning dwelling. Anon the discharge of musketry came ringing through

laden, ceased; and a stillness, nearly as fearful in its suggestiveness, followed. The bitter wind had changed from a dismal moan, to more furious blasts. The cold and damp benumbed the limbs of the wanderers, and a new danger confronted them.

"Ben," said the mother, "we must have a fire; or the children will freeze to death! I can hardly keep Amy awake."

"Do you think it will be safe?"

the forest, making the children cling more closely to their protectors. Poor little outcasts, the fatigue was telling on them! The tired, little, sunny head would drop upon the mother's shoulder, only to be rudely awakened by some distant sounds of death and destruction. The boy still trudged bravely by their sides.

It was after midnight. The awful din with which the night air had been

"Safe or not, we must have one. Come, here is a protected spot with plenty of underbrush."

Close by the gnarled roots of an oak, Ben cleared an opening, and gathering a heap of dry brush proceeded to build a fire. Then he gathered a pile of dry leaves and spread them against the tree, and as they warmed their chilly bodies, the children dropped to sleep and

Ill: CCA Christensen, detail from "Leaving Missouri" (1878), Brigham Young University Museum of Art.

were laid on their leafy bed. Ben laid his coat over them for a covering, then busied himself keeping the fire supplied with fuel while the mother kept watch over her sleeping babies. So the few remaining hours of the night passed.

Ere the light in the east had fairly reached them, the exiles were again on the march. They could not remain in the woods longer. They must try to find somebody, try to reach some place of safety. Perchance they would meet a friend, find some human being who had yet a spark of charity in his breast. So boldly out upon the open prairie they strode. But alas! vain hope, for there they found—friends? Yes, many of them. Friends by the score; but none could give them food, or clothing, or rest. They had none themselves. None could offer them protection; they too had been driven from their homes. All that they could give them, and that could be given in return, was their sympathy, their love, their faith, their prayers to God. Oh the sight, the pitiful sight, that met their eyes! There were men, women and children. Mothers driven from their worldly all, most of them without the protecting aid of husbands; some with babies, tiny babies, wrapped in coats and shawls, and pressed closely to the breast; some with a troupe of children, but there was no merriment in their faces. Some had

lost their children, they had been separated in the excitement of the mobbing, and were now wandering from one group to another, parents and children seeking each other. Ben saw a few boys like himself, helping all they could; a few able-bodied men, a very few for such a crowd of helpless beings to rely on for protection, were there. Some even of these few were disabled by bullet-rend or saber cut; while others were suffering the agonies of backs bruised by the clubs and switches of the mob. Aged grandfathers were there, grey-headed grandmothers, tottering as they bent beneath the double weight of age and persecution. Children were crying from cold; children crying for bread; children leaving the traces of their bare feet, not only with imprint, but with blood; bare-footed, bare-headed children; youths and maidens, all without proper clothing, hungry, weary from marching, and fleeing through wood and over plain, sick from injury and

Ill: CCA Christensen, detail from "Mobbers on the Missouri" (1878), Brigham Young University Museum of Art.

exposure, and faint from overwork, all pressing on to that dark boiling river whose waters roll on to the sea; leaving behind them their newly made homes, their fields, their gardens, their barns, their cattle, their all. Oh, it was a sight to make the soul sick! To make it cry out to God in anguish, to draw out the innermost heart for the suffering innocent, and to weep for the hardened, blackened soul of the persecutor.

After a great deal of toil and exposure, Ben and his little company, with others of the Saints reached the Missouri River, over which they hoped to cross and find safety and friends. A great many were there before them, and the shore was lined with campers. Some had tents; others had hastily thrown together logs in the form of huts, while still others had built a fire in the open air, around which they were sitting. The threatened storm had come and it was raining steadily. Ben secured protection for the mother and children in a tent, and joined a group at one of the fires which was struggling for life against the rain.

That evening Ben went up the river to gather fuel. He ventured a long distance, as wood was a little scarce near by. As he was about to lift his load to his shoulder, he heard the click of a fire arm and a voice in the darkness commanding him to halt.

"Nor utter a squeak," a figure said, as with some companions they surrounded him and took him prisoner.

"Are you one of the campers down on the river?" Ben was asked.

"Yes sir."

"What do you say boys, will he do?" the speaker asked of the party.

One of the men came up to Ben and peered into his face. "He's rather young, but he's better than none. You remember we vowed to flog one of them before they could leave," he said, while another added sarcastically, "'Twouldn't do fur gentlemen to break their word like that, ye know."

This seemed conclusive logic, and Ben was told to march, the mobbers poking him with their muskets.

At the sound of the word flog, Ben shuddered. Were they going to whip him, abuse him, and leave him as he had seen others left? He would ask them to kill him rather than suffer thus. The thought harrassed him, till a cold perspiration broke over him. If he could only have a chance, if he could fight what a relief it would be; but that was out of the question.

After marching about a mile from the river camp, the party halted by the side of a small grove of timber. Here they proceeded to fasten Ben's hands and feet with some hempen cords, which, it seemed, had been secured for this purpose; from his wrists, the cord was passed around a stout maple limb, and he was drawn up to it and securely fastened. Thus far, Ben had said nothing. After getting over his first fright, he lost all sense of fear, and made up his mind to take his punishment without flinching if he could. This will not appear strange when it is remembered that Ben had been surrounded for the last few days with the sufferings of women and children. He had seen them bear the greatest afflictions with fortitude. He had seen so much in fact, that it had roused within him a wonderful courage in facing the outrages that were being committed.

When Ben had been secured to the tree and his captors were stripping his back, he spoke for the first time.

"I ask you, sirs, for what am I to undergo this outrage? What crime have I committed?"

One of the men was about to answer, when the leader interrupted him with—"Do not parley with the young dog. He's not worth the breath."

"Then sir," replied Ben, "I would that you dispatch me with a bullet. I prefer it to being beaten to death."

Ben received no answer. A number of lithe hickory withes were now produced, and one of the men detailed to do the flogging. The storm had abated. The heavy clouds would now and then break open, revealing a streak of dark, blue heaven in which twinkled a star; it seemed to gaze but for a moment and then was gone; but who can tell what, in that moment, it saw; what it took cognizance of to bear witness before an eternal judgment seat!

In the awful suspense of the moment, Ben's thoughts went back to the camp on the river, and he wondered what would become of the people. From there his mind flew back over the track of his life, and his whole career was laid before him. Wonderful, in a few moments of time he lived for years!

But now the switch was ready, and as the wielder swung it around his head, it sang and shrieked in the air. The suspense now became terrible. His head be gan to swim. A film came before his eyes; and as he heard the descending instrument of torture, his feet seemed to leave the earth, and his body to float in space. A mist enclosed him—how dark—how dark it was!

Heavens! what a jolt! Benjamin South awoke with a start that nearly upset him, grandma's rocking chair, and all. Ben was trembling from head to foot. The fire in the grate had burned down and its flames had ceased their pranks. It took Ben some time to come to the realization of his senses; but when he had taken a rock or two in the chair, and found for a certainty that he was at home sitting safely in grandmother's chair what a sweet joy stole over him!

How thankful he was! Thankful? Why, that doesn't half express his joy and gratitude! His mother and Gertie and the rest came home just then from the party, and it opened their eyes to see him sitting all alone without any fire; and presto, the sullen scowl was gone, and in place a smile so cheering that it reached the whole company. Then his actions! Why they were ridiculous and really frightened the folks. He kissed his mother, seized Gertie and went dancing round the room, shook hands with George, and straightway began hugging Brother and Sister Olsen, who could do nothing but stand and laugh till their sides acked!

"Don't ask me any question," he fairly shouted, as they began plying him with queries, "I'll tell you all to-morrow."

Next day as Ben finished his narrative to the interested home circle, he said to Gertie:

"Now, sister, whenever I begin to complain and grumble about my hard, hard lot, just remind me of what I have been telling you, will you?"

Gertie promised, with pleasure.

Then turning to grandma, ever busy with her needles, he continued: "Grandma, I believe you bewitched that chair of yours last night for my special benefit, as my whole trip was taken in it. I won't be so anxious to sit in it after this, as I would rather hear you tell, or read for myself, about the Missouri persecutions, than go through the reality."

Originally published in The Contributor, *vol. 11, no. 7 (1890).*

NEPHI ANDERSON was a prominent Utah novelist during what scholars call the "Home Literature" period of Latter-day Saint writing. He published ten novels including the bestselling *Added Upon* (1898), which follows its characters from the premortal life to their final reward and can thus be regarded as the predecessor of the popular 1970s play *Saturday's Warrior*. Anderson also wrote numerous short stories, poetry, essays, and a history of the Church for young people.

KENT LARSEN is obsessed with finding obscure and forgotten Mormon literature. In near retirement, he is a graduate student in English at Hunter College in New York City.

Fiction

ASLAN OR QSLAN?
Insights into Latter-day Saint Cosmology from the Sci-fi/Fantasy Divide

JEFFREY THAYNE
AND JACOB ROSS

IMAGINE, IF YOU WILL, that you are watching an episode of a mythical ninth season of *Star Trek: The Next Generation*. The starship *Enterprise* orbits an unusual planet that is populated by some scattered humanoid civilizations at a medieval stage of technological development and a thriving community of talking animals, centaurs, and dwarfs. These animals and mythological creatures worship a benevolent talking lion they call Aslan, who—in the climatic scene of the episode—appears to the crew of the *Enterprise*. He commends Captain Jean-Luc Picard for his ethical leadership, gently scolds Commander Riker (for something or other), and has a reassuring conversation with Data.

Of course, Picard and his crew discover that this quasi-divine figure is a member of the Q—which, in Star Trek canon, are a near omnipotent race of beings that, with a snap of their fingers, can reconfigure reality to their whims. This particular Q has taken the form of a lion, populated the planet with talking animals, and behaves indistinguishably from the character in CS Lewis's story. To differentiate him from Aslan, let's call him Qslan.

The question this hypothetical episode raises for its viewers is this: *Is Qslan the same thing as Aslan?* He has the form of (and behaves indistinguishably from) Aslan. *Is that enough?*

Our answer is no (and we suspect yours is too). The universe in which Aslan is the moral sovereign of Narnia is simply not the same universe in which Jean-Luc Picard commands the *Enterprise*. Any encounter with a Q pretending to be Aslan is and will always be just that: a mimicry. Further, any encounter between Captain Picard and the *real* and *actual* Aslan would fundamentally change the Star Trek universe: it would no longer be Star Trek, but only an alt-universe mimicry of it.

We think this situation is a good proxy for why some people reject Latter-day Saints' claims to be Christian. In their minds, our Jesus talks like their Jesus, acts like their Jesus, but is, like Qslan, a mimicry. To understand why (and why Qslan isn't Aslan), it is useful to understand what makes the Star Trek universe fundamentally different from the Narnia universe—and what makes

science fiction different from fantasy, on a fundamental level.

Most will agree that the differences between science fiction and fantasy extend far deeper than aesthetics (dragons and castles vs. aliens and spaceships). Some might argue that science fiction involves plausible extrapolations of known science (the possible), while fantasy deals with the impossible. But this explanation fails because science fiction often deals with the impossible too (perhaps faster-than-light travel). All speculative fiction is counterfactual fiction—fiction that assumes the world is different than what it currently is. For example, speculative fiction may assume that the earth is flat, or that the year is 2120, or that the Nazis won World War II. However, science fiction assumes a particular *kind* of universe, while fantasy assumes another. Science fiction consists of the subset of speculative fiction set in a naturalistic universe, whereas fantasy is a subset of speculative fiction set in a non-naturalistic universe.

Science Fiction's Naturalistic World

A naturalistic universe is one in which the operations of the universe are reducible to (1) inert matter, energy, or space-time, which are (2) governed by universal rules. Purpose, meaning, and language exist in a naturalistic universe, but they are inherently *emergent* properties, ultimately reducible to more fundamental arrangements of matter and energy passively complying with universal law. Historian and philosopher Richard Carrier refers to these emergent properties as "mental things" (the type of things we associate with the human mind), and explains, "'Naturalism' means, in the simplest terms, that every mental thing is entirely caused by fundamentally nonmental things, and is entirely dependent on nonmental things for its existence."* The rules that govern a naturalistic universe, like gravity, have these specific characteristics:

- They are **universal**. If a rule varies across time and space, naturalism assumes that there is a more fundamental natural law that accounts for that change. The law of gravity holds everywhere.

- They are **unchangeable**. They cannot be altered or tweaked. They are what they must be. The law of gravity never changes, never began, will never end.

- They are **passive**. They can only await discovery. They unfold as they must, and intend nothing at all. The law of gravity just exists, wanting nothing at all.

- They are **impartial**. The physical world will run the way it runs, whether or not we are there to witness it and no matter who we are. The law of gravity does not care about your lineage or your team jersey.

- They are **morally neutral**. The universe and its rules are neither good nor bad. Morality exists only in the minds of the beings who live there. The law of gravity makes no moral judgment and is neither good nor bad.

---

* Richard Carrier, "Defining Naturalism: The Definitive Account," *Richard Carrier Blogs*, February 7, 2025, https://www.richardcarrier.info/archives/33004.

Because a naturalistic universe is passive and impartial, unfolding the laws of nature is a matter of process. Anyone who conducts similar experiments under similar conditions with sufficient skill can achieve similar results. Success in a naturalistic universe relies entirely on method, genius, and luck, not heritage, intention, or morality—the universe does not care who attempts to unlock its secrets, or what we intend to do with our knowledge.

Science fiction describes the intersection between speculative fiction and this kind of naturalistic world-building, where the imagined world follows the rules of a naturalistic world. Speculative fiction that does *not* take place in a naturalistic world is not science fiction. Further, non-speculative fiction that *does* take place in a naturalistic world is not science fiction either—it could, for example, be a romance, a mystery, or a thriller. But when speculative fiction meets naturalistic world-building, we have science fiction.

It should be noted that naturalism does not have a monopoly on science broadly speaking. Science involves rational analysis coupled with systematic observation, but it does not require that the world look the way we describe above. Those living in a non-naturalistic world might find rational analysis and systematic observation to be equally powerful tools for exploring the naturalistic parts of their world.

Science *fiction*, however, has evolved so that today its contours are almost entirely coextensive with those of naturalism. If any one of the above characteristics is violated—except, perhaps, at the

> **When speculative fiction meets naturalistic world-building, we have science fiction.**

fringes of the story and with the implication that anomalies may eventually be reducible to naturalistic formulas—the work of fiction is likely to not be treated as science fiction. People will add caveats to it, such as "science fantasy" or "science fiction with fantasy elements." This is true even if the story has the aesthetics of science fiction (such as *Star Wars*).

Nothing about this definition requires that the laws of a science fiction universe resemble our own. In fact, in many science fiction universes, they don't. Consider transporters and warp drives of Star Trek, which don't operate according to any known scientific rules. In science fiction, the rules can be different from what we know or think to be true about the world, as long as they are universal, unchangeable, passive, impartial, and morally neutral.

Lest you think we are being pedantic, we are not making this argument prescriptively per se. Rather, this perspective dovetails with the intuitions of ordinary consumers of science fiction and fantasy. Whether readers or viewers have the vocabulary to describe this distinction, many already implicitly embrace it. For example, many objected when Qui-Gon Jinn first described the existence of tiny microorganisms (midichlorians) living in the cells of "force-sensitive" people. We think viewers were intuitively noticing a shift in the fundamental character of the Star Wars universe, from a non-naturalistic one (in which the Force was an active, partial, morally inflected piece of the universe) to a more naturalistic one (in which the force could be explained by symbiosis with microorganisms). Whether this definition of science fiction is good or useful is perhaps secondary to the observation that audience members are actively using it.

Fantasy's Non-naturalistic World

In contrast with science fiction, the rules of a fantasy universe can (1) violate any of the characteristics of the rules of a naturalistic universe, and (2) interact directly with things that aren't reducible to inert matter. For example, fantasy can involve non-inert things at the substrate of the universe: the world of purpose, intention, or language can be baked into the universe itself. Or, as Carrier puts it, "at least some mental things cannot be reduced to nonmental things." Carrier provides some clear examples of how this might work:

> In Harry Potter's world, a wizard speaks a word and something happens. A single word causes a wand to generate light, another word causes objects to move wherever the wand points, and so on. ... In a similar fashion, in the novel *Jonathan Strange & Mr. Norrell* (now a miniseries), the rocks and trees and winds respond to verbal commands, despite having no brains or ears or nervous systems, *or anything structurally analogous to these.* Therefore, magic in the Harry Potter and Jonathan Strange universes ... relies on

> **A fantasy universe is active rather than passive; it responds rather than merely reacts.**

irreducibly mental powers and properties of the universe. Words *directly* cause what they request, without any mindless mechanism connecting the spoken word to the realized effect.*

This concept could include the animism present in some fantasy worlds. For example, a mountain itself might seek to repel trespassers (e.g., Cahadras in *Lord of the Rings*). The stars themselves might join in the battle between good and evil (*A Wrinkle in Time*).

In other words, a fantasy universe is active rather than passive; it *responds* rather than merely reacts. As Neil Postman puts it, there is an "irrevocable difference between a blink and a wink,"† and a fantasy universe can do the latter. Further, fantasy can defy each of the characteristics of the rules of naturalism:

- **In fantasy, the rules of the universe can vary across space**, without there necessarily being a universal rule underneath to explain the changes. You could have cursed communities or enchanted forests or sacred relics where the rules are just different.

- **In fantasy, the rules of the universe can vary across time.** The magic can die, or reawaken.

You could have a magician create magic, or deities that rewrite the rules.

- **In fantasy, the rules or forces of the universe can be active.** They might have intention. The magic might seek out the magician as much as the magician seeks out the magic.

- **In fantasy, the rules or magic of the universe can be partial.** It might matter *who* is trying to seek out the universe's secret, and what they intend it for. Heritage and family might matter.

- **In fantasy, the rules or magic of the universe can be morally inflected.** You can have good magic that enchants and uplifts, or dark magic that inevitably corrupts and destroys. Goodness and badness can be baked into the universe.

Fantasy does not need to do *all* of these things (or necessarily any specific one of them), but each signals to a reader that we are dealing with a non-naturalistic universe and are therefore likely in the realm of fantasy.

Some mistakenly assume that this means that a fantasy universe *cannot* have rules that are systematic.

---

* Carrier, "Defining Naturalism."

† Neil Postman, "Social Science as Theology," *ETC: A Review of General Semantics* 41, no. 1 (Spring 1984): 22–32.

However, the rules of allomancy in the Mistborn series by Brandon Sanderson are heavily systematized but are also non-naturalistic. For example (spoiler alert!), the rules are changeable: they were created by a dying god in an attempt to distribute his creative power through the world. Magic does not have to be *mysterious* to be magic. It just has to violate one or more of the characteristics of naturalism.

Applications for Writers

This distinction between genres can help writers establish their work as science fiction or fantasy, which can shift the entire "vibe" of their work. If an author is aiming for the more enchanted flavor of fantasy, they might include animistic elements in their story. Jim Butcher's *The Aeronaut's Windlass* was a strong contender for alt-universe science fiction with its counterfactual physics and levitation crystals, until the characters discover that their airship (the Predator) is *alive* and can converse with mystics among its crew—the ship is animistic in a way that may be hard to reduce to naturalistic rules. No matter how naturalistic the universe might appear, this animism gives the story its enchanted flavor.

Further, authors might use these ideas to make good and bad more than just a team jersey. In Brandon Sanderson's *Words of Radiance*, we see magic used in highly sophisticated, technological ways: gems filled with stormlight are used in engineered devices to create effects not otherwise possible. However, not only is there animism involved in the story (the spren), the characters' ability to tap into the vast powers offered by the spren is contingent on their moral character. Kaladin lost his abilities for a while because he betrayed an oath that he had made. Another way to use this technique is to make good and evil baked into the cosmology of the world. For example, imagine a colony of spacefarers who must morally recenter themselves in order to advance on their pilgrimage through space, because otherwise things go awry. Even if everything that goes wrong (or right!) has a perfectly naturalistic explanation, the fact that their progress becomes contingent on their moral character signals that they don't live in an impartial universe, which can give the otherwise science fiction story an enchanted feel.

But perhaps even more useful, these distinctions can help ensure that authors do not inadvertently *dis*enchant their worlds, as George Lucas did when he introduced mid-ichlorians. Some writers mistakenly assume that, in order to systematize their magic, they must systematize it in a naturalistic way. For example, the forest is enchanted because of unobtanium deposits in the ground, the magic appears partial to a particular lineage because of genetic differences or parasites, or "dark magic" is revealed to simply be entropy by another name. In other words, writers can—almost like the Borg from Star Trek—assimilate non-naturalistic premises into naturalistic premises. None of that is bad in and of itself: authors are certainly allowed to disenchant their universes. It is only a problem when it's done unintentionally, or when writers do not fully understand why readers and viewers actually love the universe they've created for them.

Is Advanced Science Indistinguishable from Theology?

Science fiction author Arthur C. Clarke famously wrote, "Any sufficiently advanced technology is indistinguishable from magic."* This idea has become central to how science fiction deals with the non-naturalistic. For example, in the *Star Trek: The Next Generation* episode "Who Watches the Watchers," a member of a primitive alien race witnesses members of the *Enterprise* crew use advanced technology and concludes that Captain Picard is a god.

Star Trek: The Next Generation,
season 3, episode 4, "Who Watches
the Watchers" (1989)

Picard responds that any advanced technology will resemble magic to less advanced civilizations. Indeed, a revision of Clarke's quote by Michael Shermer reads, "Any sufficiently advanced extraterrestrial intelligence is indistinguishable from God."†

However, is this principle true? Teleportation in Star Trek is functionally equivalent to apparition in the Harry Potter universe. Both allow people to move instantaneously from one location to another, and through barriers, with absolute ease. And yet few Star Trek fans think of the *Enterprise*'s transporter system as magic, and few Harry Potter fans consider apparating to be a technology. Although they look similar, consumers of science fiction and fantasy intuitively understand that they are different on a fundamental level.

---

* Arthur C. Clarke, *Profiles of the Future: An Inquiry into the Limits of the Possible* (Harper & Row, 1973), 21.

† Michael Shermer, "Shermer's Last Law," *Scientific American*, January 2002.

In other words, sufficiently advanced technology can be distinguished from magic, at least in concept. Technology produces extraordinary results in a naturalistic universe, and magic produces extraordinary results in a non-naturalistic universe. The difference is not in the teleportation, but in the kind of universe it takes place in. As Carrier explains, "Clarke's Third Law ('any sufficiently advanced technology is indistinguishable from magic') is only,

Aslan is *goodness itself*. As the moral sovereign of his universe, Aslan is an animistic embodiment of the powers that be. If the true Aslan were to appear on the *Enterprise*, either the Star Trek universe would become morally inflected in a way that is foreign to its naturalistic premises and history, or Narnia would become merely one alien world among many, and Aslan would become simply an uber-benevolent and powerful alien, who merely resembled in many

Sufficiently advanced technology can be distinguished from magic.

at best, an *epistemological* principle, not a metaphysical one. Metaphysically, magic and technology are very definitely always distinguishable."*

Which brings us to our point: Qslan is not the same as Aslan, and he is easily distinguishable from Aslan. Qslan lives in a naturalistic universe. He inherited his powers from predecessors who studied a passive, impartial, and morally neutral universe and unraveled its mysteries. There's nothing baked into a naturalistic universe that requires Qslan to be benevolent. In contrast, good and evil are baked into the fabric of the Narnia universe. Aslan does not merely *happen* to be good,

respects the Aslan of Narnia. In this way, the naturalism of Star Trek would infect Aslan's very nature in ways that make him *no longer Aslan*. He would be a different being going by the same name.

This conclusion brings us back to some of the grievances that some Christians have with Latter-day Saints. Joseph Smith taught, "God himself, finding he was in the midst of spirits and glory, because he was more intelligent, saw proper to institute laws whereby the rest could have privilege to advance like himself." †Further, Latter-day Saints do not see God as an abstract entity, but as a physical, embodied person with flesh

---

* Carrier, "Defining Naturalism."
† Joseph Smith, "The King Follett Discourse," *Ensign*, May 1971.

and bones. Joseph Smith revealed, "The Father has a body of flesh and bones as tangible as man's" (D&C 130:22). Elder Parley P. Pratt wrote:

> What is God? He is material, organized intelligence, possessing both body and parts. He is in the form of man, and is in fact of the same species; and is a [model], or standard of perfection to which man is destined to attain; he being the great father, and head of the whole family. He can go, come, converse, reason, eat, drink, love, hate, rejoice, possess and enjoy.‡

Similarly, President Lorenzo Snow wrote the famous couplet, "As man is, God once was; as God is, man may become."§ Some Christians hear this as just another iteration of Clarke's third law: God's power is mere technological mastery in disguise. They may interpret this to mean that for Latter-day Saints God is just part of a more advanced civilization of beings that understands the universe better than we do, cosmic aliens populating our planet with beings to worship them. And, as a result, they see our doctrine as offering Qslan instead of Aslan.

For some Christians, the Latter-day Saint perspective disenchants the universe and perhaps even changes the *genre* of the unfolding narrative of the faith: it is, in their minds, a worldview more fit for science fiction than the Christian universe given to us by Paul and the apostles. We have seen Latter-day Saints embrace a similar view of their own faith (though rarely articulating it directly). We have indeed heard some Latter-day Saints argue that all of God's power is obtained through purely naturalistic means and is based on rules that are fundamentally naturalistic in nature and character.

Non-naturalism Matters to Latter-day Saint Thought

It is to this group of Latter-day Saints that we are writing. Perhaps they are eager to reconcile revealed truth with the naturalism that is the default of current scientific inquiry. Perhaps they have read statements from Church leaders or thinkers that they interpret to have implied this. Either way, they have arrived at the conclusion that the universe, in its fundamentals, operates naturalistically—and that God is able to operate as God by virtue of His scientific and technological advancement (or, failing that, some evolutionary advancement).

---

‡ Benjamin E. Park and Jordan T. Watkins, "The Riches of Mormon Materialism: Parley P. Pratt's 'Materiality' and Early Mormon Theology," *Mormon Historical Studies* 11 (2010): 159–72.

§ Gerald N. Lund, "Is President Lorenzo Snow's Oft-Repeated Statement—'As Man Now Is, God Once Was; as God Now Is, Man May Be'—Accepted as Official Doctrine by the Church?" *Ensign*, February 1982.

Our argument is simple: we also think that Qslan isn't Aslan, and that God should not be thought of as Qslan. We don't worship some alien-god pretending to be our moral sovereign. Put differently, we think that Latter-day Saint cosmology is fundamentally *non*-naturalistic, and that a cursory read of our scriptures bears that out. We could make a larger case for this if this were an academic or theological treatise, but it is not—we are here simply to draw some connections between genre analysis and those broader discussions. But we will briefly state two reasons why we believe LDS theology relies on a non-naturalistic worldview.

First, we believe in a morally inflected universe. We see good and evil as baked into the fabric of the universe, and not merely a matter of preference or convention. In the Latter-day Saint view—as far as we understand it—God is not God by virtue of His technological skill, but by virtue of His moral perfection. There is no way to step into God's power and authority except by stepping into the kind of moral character He embodies. If God advanced to His current station (and if we might advance similarly), it was through moral advancement and character formation, not some cosmological engineering degree. God isn't a technologically advanced being who just happens to be good.

For Latter-day Saints, God being flesh and bones makes him no less a moral authority than the fact that Aslan had paws and teeth. A bold implication of the restored Gospel is that God's moral authority does not require God's fundamental otherness or that God be the unmoved mover of heaven and earth. The universe can still be fundamentally morally inflected, even if we have a divine heritage and destiny as God's children and join-heirs with Christ.

Second, we live in a fundamentally animistic universe. For Latter-day Saints, intelligence, life, creation are not mere emergent properties of a fundamentally lifeless substrate. In fact, the very claims of our doctrine that are at issue hold that mankind is co-eternal with God, that our intelligences are neither created nor emergent but part of the bedrock substrate of the universe. And many Latter-day Saints believe that we are not wholly alone; many argue that the universe is not merely reactive to the activities of God, but responsive to them. In other words, as Lehi put it, there are in the universe "things to act and things to be acted upon" (2 Nephi 2:14), and the former is not derived from the latter. We are not mere meat machines enacting our genetic and environmental programming—at our center there is something fundamentally agentic. There is more to the universe than inert matter following naturalistic laws. Moral agency, will, intention are bedrock, not emergent from or reducible to fundamentally inert processes. There is something *alive* within and about the universe we live in.

Put in the most plain words, the *actual* universe we live in is non-naturalistic, even if pieces of it behave naturalistically. None of this bridges the other theological differences between Latter-day Saints and other Christians, nor do we intend to bridge those differences. Our argument is simply that Latter-day Saints broadly view the universe as *enchanted* in many of the same ways assumed in fantasy worldbuilding rather than science fiction worldbuilding. And if we become too enamored of naturalism as we discuss our theological differences, we can inadvertently disenchant the universe in the process.

Disenchantment is one of the ongoing themes of Star Trek. Time and again, mysteries that appear divine or magical are—by the episode's end—reduced to advanced technology or misunderstood science. In *The Original Series* episode "Who Mourns for Adonais?", the crew meets a being who claims to be Apollo. They dismiss him as merely a powerful alien pretending to be a god. In *The Next Generation* episodes "Who Watches the Watchers?" and "Devil's Due," godlike figures are similarly unveiled as products of technology or deception. Across the franchise, the arc bends toward disenchantment: the universe is continually demystified, rendered always in naturalistic terms.

Rather than doing the same to our own God, we think some re-enchantment is in order—both in our theologizing and in our storytelling. The mood of what we are talking about is best captured by works like C. S. Lewis's Space Trilogy or Madeleine L'Engle's *A Wrinkle in Time*. On the surface, both stories use the props of science fiction—spaceships, extraterrestrial worlds, time travel, scientific language. But beneath these trappings, their universes are not naturalistic at all. They are morally inflected and alive with agency at every level. In Lewis's *Out of the Silent Planet*, for example, the eldila (angelic beings) are woven into the very fabric of the cosmos, and every planet is governed by its own Oyarsa, a spiritual ruler whose authority is not reducible to physics or biology. In *A Wrinkle in Time*, the great struggle between good and evil is not an incidental byproduct of blind natural law, but the central drama of the universe itself, with stars and angels alike joining the fight.

These stories remind us that science fiction aesthetics do not have to imply a naturalistic universe. These stories can be vehicles for imagining worlds where meaning, intention, and goodness are bedrock realities rather than emergent illusions—and we invite Latter-day Saint fiction writers to write more of them. Why can't Starship captains pray? Why can't space exploration be imbued with *moral* purpose? Further, these stories echo more closely the Latter-day Saint view of the universe we actually inhabit: a cosmos that is at once orderly and alive, rationally intelligible yet fundamentally moral and responsive.

Of course, there are no ultimate contradictions between religion and science—but this does not mean that we need to embrace the naturalism that is the default of current scientific inquiry. Empirical observation and rational analysis do not bend inexorably towards a naturalistic view of the universe: naturalism is a pragmatic but pre-empirical lens. Nothing requires that we wear it, and especially not at all times and in all places.

In short, we do not live in a Star Trek universe, however much of it may look that way on the surface. We inhabit a universe that is morally inflected and alive with agency, intention, and meaning. For us, the Restoration is not a naturalistic retelling of Christianity, but, from Lehi to Joseph Smith, a bold reassertion that the universe itself is more akin to Narnia than to the world of Starfleet. To forget this is to risk rewriting the genre of our own faith.

Dr. JEFFREY THAYNE graduated from BYU with a bachelor's and master's degree in psychology. He completed his doctorate in Instructional Technology and Learning Sciences at Utah State University. He spends time engaging in worldview apologetics (articulating and exploring the worldview assumptions that inform our faith). He currently resides in Rexburg, Idaho with his wife and two children, and teaches at Brigham Young University-Idaho.

JACOB ROSS is an analyst with degrees in Mathematics and Economics from Brigham Young University. A lifelong consumer of science fiction and fantasy, he yearns for a day when he can write in both genres simultaneously and at the same time transmit timeless gospel truths through his stories.

Poetry

DEATH

CAROL LYNN PEARSON

Death is the great forget, they said,
A mindless, restful leaving
Of all consciousness and care
In a vast unweaving.

And so I waited, cramped and still,
For approaching Death to bring
Forgetfulness—but all he brought
Was a huge remembering.

Originally published in Dialogue: A Journal of Mormon Thought, *vol. 1, no.*
2 (1966).

CAROL LYNN PEARSON has been a professional writer, speaker and performer for many years, devoted to transforming patriarchy into partnership. Her memoir, *Goodbye, I Love You*, tells the story of her marriage to a homosexual man, their divorce, ongoing friendship, and her caring for him as he died of AIDS. Her work transcends religious and cultural boundaries and she continues to work within the Mormon community, the religion of her pioneer ancestors. She has an MA in theater and lives in Walnut Creek, California.

Fiction

THE MOTHERS

CHANEL EARL

WE ARE THE mothers without children, the ones of whom it is written that *once upon a time, there was a woman, and more than anything, she wanted a child.*

We are bakers' and farmers' wives. We are witches and queens. We are young, almost children ourselves. We are lonely old maids. We are rich. We are starving.

We do work that brings us honor and work that nobody notices. We nurture and encourage, cook and clean, sew and sing. We keep gardens of beans and rampion and make cake for angels delivering heavenly messages. We go to the temple and make our sacrifices. We discover hidden secrets.

We hold other women's children, then lie awake at night weeping.

We blame the men in our lives. They should marry us. They should have sex with us. We chastise our husbands because they cannot father children. Their curse is ours. We blame their sins, their diets, their parents. We blame the weather.

We blame ourselves, seeing every weakness and failure. We waited too long, didn't think of the consequences of our decisions. We have the wrong genes, the wrong health. We are broken and don't deserve children. We are monsters.

When we prick our fingers, we wish for a child with lips red as blood. When we see a branch or a root in the shape of a child, we take

Ill: JJ Grandville, Pansy from The Flowers Personified (1847)

it home and call it our baby. We seek blessings from kings and prophets. We go to doctors, drink elixirs, and eat anything that we are told to eat: eggs, yams, nuts, bones, figs. We eat only those. We do whatever it takes.

We blame God. We hate God. We love God. We turn to God, to gods, fasting and praying for children to fill the empty space inside of us even as we grow more hollow. We pray all night and day. We make bargains, visit witches who cast spells and share secrets, quest through woods and fields. We wish on all of the stars and make promises we will be forced to keep.

We will never be satisfied until we have children. We know women who have no children, who choose it, women who are *happy* without children. We decide to be like them. We remind ourselves that children are costly. They would keep us awake. They would destroy our bodies, impoverish us, break our hearts. We tell ourselves that we are the lucky ones and that mothers *with* children are cursed.

We try, but don't believe it.

The children never come, so we give our love to all who will take it. We build things that we love and call them our children. We kidnap other women's children and lock them in towers. We make animals our babies. We become witches, learning magic that goes beyond that of the pretend witches we visited when we were in need, the ones that never helped us.

To some, children do come, unexpectedly, when we are so old we have given up all hope, when the thought of a child being born to us makes us laugh. To others, they come immediately after the promises we made so desperately. Our husbands can't believe it. They are struck dumb or are long dead. They are in awe of us and our miracles. They weep with joy and sadness.

Some of us give birth to our children screaming. Some find our children in baskets floating on the river or tucked neatly into the petals of blooming flowers. We make our children, carved of wood or formed of clay. We plant them and watch their contorted faces grow. We bake them in our ovens, trusting that they will come to life, birthed from the heat.

We may die as our children come into the world, knowing that our sacrifice was for a purpose. We are happy to give our lives to bring our children into reality, and we are devastated that our time with them was so short. *What justice is*

Ill: JJ Grandville, Poppy from The Flowers Personified (1847) this, we ask our God, *that our long-sought children enter the world just as we leave it?* Our husbands raise our children alone.

Others live. Our children are the size of a thumb. They sleep in walnut shells and wash their faces with dew drops. They are carried off by birds and toads before we have a chance to mother them. They are taken from us, hidden underneath the skins of animals, or locked in other mothers' towers. They run away. They are carried away by God, taken to temples to become prophets and never cut their hair. They advise kings and baptize kings of kings. They see visions, sire nations, and lose their heads in the service of their God.

Or we see our children become monsters. They are half-animal, cruel, and strange. They are golems and shades. They can't speak. They cry all the time. They are endlessly hungry, eating all of the food in our houses before eating us and our neighbors and entire herds of cattle and swine.

Our children are cursed. They lose their gravity, or they wax and wane with the moon. They are sent away for their protection. We burn every spinning wheel in the kingdom to save them. We lie awake at night worrying about them, and even when we can't remember what they looked like, the beautiful sounds of their voices echo in our lonely ears.

We thought that our children were part of our stories, but our stories are finished. We fade from view as our children's stories come into focus. Even when we live to see them lead nations from bondage, call fire from the sky, find true love, or wake from a hundred-year sleep, they outlive us. They break their curses, shed their animal skins, and leave us behind, going on to carry our magic and hope into new stories.

And we become footnotes, single lines at the beginnings of their tales: *Once upon a time, there was a woman, and more than anything else, she wanted a child.*

CHANEL EARL is a Pushcart Prize and Best of the Net–nominated writer of short fiction and essays. She has an MFA in creative writing from Brigham Young University, where she teaches writing to undergraduates. Her stories and essays have appeared in such publications as *Smokelong Quarterly*, *Granfalloon*, *The Account*, and *Wayfare Magazine*.

Ill: JJ Grandville, Marguerite from The Flowers Personified (1847)

THE ENEMY HAS A BODY
A Confidential Memo
DISCOVERED BY JORDAN LAKE

My beloved Bilewort,

YOUR REPORT ON YOUR PATIENT'S anger towards his university has brought a smile to my face. He has been long overdue for an angry episode. The frustration of both your man and the counselor led to a most deliciously unproductive meeting, where both left the appointment complaining to their respective friends and family about the unreasonableness of the other. As you know, encourage your patient to associate this one bad experience with their overall view of the university. The residual aggravation will be delicious to your tongue, my Niece.

Of course, I have not only written to congratulate you. No. I have written to you with more dire intent, and to keep you on the lookout for upcoming changes to our duties. I believe we have fallen for our own propaganda. Yes, I know. I can see your look of disbelief as I am writing to you now. The truth shall soon be sent out abroad by our superiors. Since you have already graduated, and no longer review the curriculum of the Tempters' Training College For Young Devils (a neglectful choice, I will add), you will not have caught the subtle shifts in our publications and research. Recent articles, published in *Beelzebub's Weekly*, point to the idea that we have misunderstood the very nature of the enemy for nearly two millennia.

In the obituary of one Blunderpug (his name says it all), a peculiar account is given that hints at our recent revelation. Having lost his patient to heaven, the account reports that while watching his patient be embraced in the arms of the enemy, Blunderpug stepped back and slipped on the beads of the patient's rosary lying on the floor. As he fell, he made direct eye contact with the enemy. The poor fool was in flames before he hit the floor. But, before his passing, came the dreadful words, "Eyebrows! Knees! And cuticles! *Both of them!*" Did this filth come from confusion and pain? Or does it hint toward truth? It is the latter, I am afraid. By this report, we believe Blunderpug saw two beings, both with tangible bodies. One was embracing the patient, the other standing nearby. Based on his description, both had specific, bodily features like the vermin. If anything came of Blunderpug's undoing, it is that he has prepared the way for the truth.

We have had many descriptions of the enemy that circle the same spiritual concept of oneness in being. Is the enemy, as the delightfully devilish Screwtape believed, to be "three as well as one?"* That is what we have believed. There have been thousands of descriptions that originated from thousands of creeds, which we *still* perpetuate. Yet there is one description that we buried two millennia ago into such depths of obscurity that even we lost sight of it. It is the idea of an embodied God, one covered in resurrected slime, and a separate person from his sleazy son.

We have long known about the son's body, believing it to be kept as an example to humans. But now we understand that it is not only for the vermin, but also to emulate His father's body. It is this view of the enemy that we have avoided. Double the embodied deity, double the headache. This is not to mention the third of the lot. The spirit that, by all accounts, speaks and tempts the vermin as we do, only to help them avoid the devilish and the immoral. The homewrecker. This trio, supposedly one in purpose, separate in being, provides new attacks that were heretofore undiagnosed by our legions of tempters.

The danger we have put ourselves in is that we currently target only one enemy, mistaking the roles of three to be the works of one. But now there are three separate beings we must steer our patients clear of. As we try to block

---

* CS Lewis, *The Screwtape Letters* (HarperOne, 2015), 94.

the attempts of one, the other two flank us from behind and secure the virtue of the patient. It's cruelty of the highest order. If tenure weren't so nearly in my grasp, I would retire.

This leads me to address your problem. Your patient already believes in the embodied enemy, and now we are one step behind. I don't blame you for this, as just yesterday we believed it to be your patients' undoing. But now, you must shift your efforts to prevent him from worshipping the three separate beings rather than encourage it. At the very least, you must obscure the differences between them so that he cannot tell one from the other.

We have always known that the enemy means to make the pests like himself. But now we realize that this goal is far more literal than we ever dreamt of. This implies that the vermin are actually the same species as the enemy. Within their very being is the same potential of the enemy, locked away from our ever being able to detract from it. Imagine the faith this knowledge could produce within any human who believes it. What's worse, these "Latter-day Saints" have preached this doctrine for almost two hundred years, and all we have done is scoff. It is time for us to start fighting back.

My first piece of advice is to steer your man away from contemplating his divine nature.

Numb his senses and thoughts through his media habits, encouraging him to endlessly listen to podcasts or other sources of entertainment. Let your patient distract himself while doing "good" things all day, never contemplating the enemy or his connection to him. Without contemplating his nature, his confidence in the enemy will wane.

Second, there is a habit of yours I want to highlight. You laugh about putting strange thoughts into your patient's mind, such as questioning whether the embodied enemy has a belly button or not. But this is no longer a laughing matter. Your patient must now be steered away from believing in a resurrected deity at all costs. Jests such as these only solidify the image of the *embodied enemy* in the mind of your patient.

My final piece of advice for now is to encourage division between the mind and body of your patient. We have always known that the spirit must overcome the body in the enemy's view. We have also always known that the enemy celebrates matter, having given his creations material body and form. But now we know that the spiritual and physical, joined together, are the ideal state of being for humans. Because of this, be sure to instill habits within your man that cause friction between his spirit and body. For example, encourage excess in food or substances (your patient, in particular, struggles with caffeine), things that neither promote nor strengthen the connection between the body and spirit. Addiction, my niece, of any kind and of any substance, draws conflict between the spirit and the body. While the body receives pleasure by satisfying the addiction, the spirit shies away.

Please keep me updated on your efforts to subvert your patients' beliefs in light of these discoveries. I'd like to help you make this transition so that your patient isn't lost to the cause of heaven. With these successes you have had, do not become full of yourself. Remember, we must exercise virtue to squelch their virtue. You must be humble to bring out the pride of your patient. Consider your relationship with your patient as symbiotic, like the bird to the hippo, or the caffeine to your patient.

I hope that you will keep my correspondence with you to yourself for the time being. These are topics not to be trifled with, and can lead to our losing many fiendish souls.

Your affectionate uncle,
GRINDLEHOOK

JORDAN LAKE is a recent graduate of Brigham Young University–Idaho, where he majored in Communications with a minor in English. He and his wife, a recent nursing graduate from BYU–I, live in Rexburg. Jordan plans to attend law school in the Fall of 2026. He loves to write religious commentary and literary analysis, and is just breaking into the market of satire.